I0571762

pineLight

pineLight

BOOK | **ONE**

JILLIAN PEERY

Cover Art by Josh Longbrake

First Ebook Edition: June, 2011
First Paperback Edition: July, 2011
Ebook ISBN: 978-0-9837507-0-3
Paperback ISBN: 978-0-9837507-2-7

To book a signing event, submit your request at www.jillianpeery.com.

First Paperback Edition
Printed in the United States of America

For my husband, Clint,
whose love and inspiration
made this dream a reality.
I love you.

For our struggle is not against flesh and blood, but against the rulers, against the authorities, against the powers of this dark world, and against the spiritual forces of evil in the heavenly realms.

—Ephesians 6:12

PREFACE
Thirty-Seven Months Ago

LIGHT FROM THE FLICKERING CANDLES SENT A STABBING PAIN through my eyes. The sound of crackling wood echoed through the hallway, and the bold aroma of smoke filled my lungs, causing me to feel nauseated. Pain was being released, and it was attacking my body. I felt it pounding in my head—a severe pain, the kind of pain that renders you helpless. It was hard to think. *How did I get here?* He had me pinned between his body and the cold stone of the wall. I blinked heavily as I tried to focus—to see into his dark eyes. My vision was distorted, and I felt strangely dizzy.

"Did you really think I wanted it to come to this? You just wouldn't let go. I gave you every opportunity—every opportunity—to leave it all behind. Why couldn't you let your love overcome your hate for me?" His jawline tightened when I didn't respond. "Don't pretend I mean nothing to you. You are tempted—I can feel it."

I stared blankly in confusion. I didn't know what to say.

"Well, there's nothing you can do now. Your precious memories are slipping away. Your fate will be sealed tonight." His voice was strong and angry, but his eyes seemed to reflect all the sadness in the world. *Why was he yelling?* I struggled to remember why he was angry. Thoughts and images were briefly appearing and disappearing, creating chaos in my mind.

He pushed me out of the lit hallway into a dark room. The blue glow of the moon seeped in through a window that was halfway tucked behind a torn curtain. Everything looked gray and grim in the moonlight. He forced my body backward onto a massive bed in the middle of the room and threw me to its silky surface. A chill came to my skin as his hand tightened around my neck.

"He wanted me to kill you, you know."

He suddenly released his grip and stormed across the room, slamming a red door behind him. I heard the metal key grind as it turned inside the rusty lock of the door, sealing me within my prison.

"I can keep you safe." His voice, now more controlled, sounded strangely anxious through the wooden cracks of the door.

The sound of pounding boots charging down the empty corridor echoed eerily through the room. There was another sharp, throbbing pain in my head. *How did this all begin? How did I get in this room?* Once again, confusion was settling in.

I carefully pulled myself to a sitting position, rubbing my pounding temple, dazed by the pain. As my eyes began to focus, I gradually became aware of a soft glow illuminating my clenched fist. I slowly unfolded each finger to reveal light emanating from a cross pendant—a pendant covered in wet blood.

Immediately, blurry images from earlier in the night flashed in my mind.

He was taking everything from me.

I frantically tied the loose ribbon of the pendant around my neck, jumped from the bed, and then rushed to the glazed window. The night sky illuminated the angry ocean as roaring waves from far below crashed and foamed around the boulders protecting the embankment of the castle. All was dark and ominous.

I knew I had to jump—it was the only way. My past would soon slip away, along with every recollection of anyone I had ever known. All of my loved ones—would be forgotten. Everything I believed in—would be lost. I would much rather plunge into the dark waters than fall victim to this malicious plan. I could never be his.

-1-

RED RIVER PARISH, LOUISIANA
PRESENT DAY

I watch as the seasons change. Leaves float in the sky and fall gracefully to the earth. I sit and wish that you were here with me. Night takes the day, and I can feel you near. I can't see your face, but I know you are in my dreams. I hear you. I wait to find you, the one who haunts my soul. Where are you? Only the seasons ever change; leaves continue to fall and then rustle about the earth. Night continues to reign over me. Though the memories are lost, I know a part of you is still with me.

-Clara

MY FIST CLASPED THE CRUMPLED PIECE OF PAPER HIDDEN tightly under my fingers. Trails of rain scattered sideways on the passenger window. I concentrated on the rain and the rapid flutter of the windshield wipers. I didn't want to think about what was happening in the cab of the truck. I didn't want to cry—not in front of him. The light tapping of raindrops steadily increased, much like the tension between us. I could feel him waiting for me to speak, but I was determined not to give him that satisfaction.

It was seventy-two degrees in Red River Parish, windy, and the clouds were releasing their dark gray fury across town. I had dressed appropriately for the dreary day, no doubt, but the dampness caused by the rain combined with the chill of the truck's blasting air conditioner was enough to make anyone uncomfortable. Instead of powering down the air or closing the vents on the dash, I shoved my hands further into my jacket pockets and leaned toward the fogged window. I didn't want him to know I was uncomfortable—I didn't want him to know anything about how I felt.

The drive to Coushatta always seemed to stretch in bad weather. The small town of nearly three thousand townspeople rested along the north side of the Red River. I lived with my Aunt Alice on the gloomy southwest side, miles from everything in Louisiana, except for the town's oldest cemetery. We had been the only living souls on this side of the parish, until a mortician and his son moved in to the vacant house at the cemetery. It was there in the quiet graveyard, under the frozen wings of stone angels, that I had met Erik.

My eyes darted over to him. The silence and our closeness made the truck seem stifling, and I found myself working harder to think, even to breathe. I couldn't believe what he had done.

Erik usually had an alluring way about him, but that trance was broken now. His eyes were hidden by the dark shade of his sunglasses, like they usually were. But I knew he was stealing glances at me. Just like I was at him. His seemingly fixated stare on the road and tight grip on the steering wheel kept my mind wandering uneasily. *How could I have trusted him?* There was a knot of embarrassment forming in my stomach.

For the first time, I hated him. I hated everything about his perfect olive skin, his deep brown eyes, even his messy hair. I hated that, for the next ten minutes, I was stuck near him, with no way out. I wanted to be as far away from him as humanly possible.

"Clara," he said in a charming voice, breaking the silence. "You can't ignore me forever."

I sighed, knowing this was partially true. Erik had an unexplainable aura that followed him everywhere, pulling everyone in—including me. There was no denying that. He knew he had this strange power over me, just like he did with everyone in the parish. But this time I saw past his charm, and I wasn't going to let him pull me back in.

"It should be easy," I snapped. I was surprised that my voice sounded strong and not shaky.

The cab of the truck was silent again, except for the hard tapping of the rain. The smooth lips I had once admired were now unnaturally pursed—he was undoubtedly searching for something to say.

"Easy. Really," he murmured, but there was a hint of a question in his tone.

I wiggled down in my seat and looked to the passenger window. The blue glow of the sky struck across the wet glass, and for a moment I could see my reflection in the haze.

My skin looked even paler on dreary days like these, and my freckles darker, especially when my hair was down against my face. I ran my fingers through the auburn tangles and pushed them behind my ears. It didn't seem to help my translucent reflection.

My eyes were still fixated on the window when we passed the sign that read: RED RIVER PARISH HIGH—Home of the Mighty Bulldogs. Through the veil of rain and gloom, our eerie Edwardian-style school sat somberly in the background, waiting for us to enter. At dawn and dusk, the light would hit the lines of the school, highlighting the beauty in its architecture. It was picturesque, but today, its beauty was masked with a gothic veil. Today everything was bleak.

The truck slowed as we took an easy turn into the back parking lot of the school, and then jolted when the wheels rolled over the first of the three familiar speed bumps. Erik immediately took a hard left, away from the school building, and slammed on the brakes. The truck came to a screeching halt under an isolated bald cypress tree that dripped with both rain and moss.

I heard him toss his shades onto the dashboard, but I kept my eyes focused ahead on the tree.

"You wish to ignore me," he said. Though it was a statement, he sounded confused.

I glanced long enough to realize he was inching his way toward me, and then shot my attention back to the tree.

"Come on, Clarabella," he continued with a grin. "That's not what you want."

His hand slid over mine, like it always did when he wanted something, but I pulled away. I felt my mind slightly spin for a moment, before realizing his grin had faded and he was studying me.

"So ripping a few entries from your journal was a bad idea. I get it," he said, releasing a heavy breath of peppermint into the air. "But surely you can get over that."

His words fueled the fire inside of me. I thought back to all the times he had been in my house—in my room. All the unintentional opportunities I had given him to go through all of my things, to steal my journal. Everything I felt, my unexplainable thoughts and emotions, were written within those pages. I was mortified he had read them. *He wants me to just get over it?* My temples pulsed.

"I want it back." I paused to correct myself. "I want back every single page."

He chuckled to himself before letting me in on his bad joke. "The only page you're going to find is the one in your hand."

"Where are the others?"

He was silent.

"Tell me, Erik!" I demanded an answer.

"Listen, Clara—forget about it. You don't need them back." His eyes were black poison when he looked at me. I couldn't look away from them. His voice buzzed in my head. "Forget about it," he repeated slowly.

My mind went fuzzy again.

Somehow I managed to tuck his words in my pocket—to shake out the buzz. My mind cleared and soared back to what I wanted. *The pages.*

"Give them to me," I demanded.

He appeared surprised by my reaction, almost irritated. I noticed his mouth tighten as if he were biting the inside of his cheek.

"Give them to me now—or never talk to me again."

He was glaring at me with sinister eyes, while his chest expanded and breath quickened. Maybe he was angry that his usual charm had failed to work, or maybe he didn't approve of my demands. Either way something had stirred him.

"I can't do that."

"Fine," I said. "I never want to see you again." I slid over to the truck door and pushed it open. I was finally free of the truck—free of him—but now I was standing with my bag in the pouring rain.

"Don't be ridiculous. Get back in the truck, Clara."

His voice faded into the sound of rain as I broke into a frantic run. It was all I could do. I ran through the old cypress trees that shadowed the cracked parking lot, and then ran some more. I ran, seemingly for miles in the rain, darting through the woods that overlooked our school. Feelings of betrayal churned inside of me. Agony and humiliation drove me. I couldn't stop. I wanted nothing more than to be numb. The rain continued to pour down through the trees, soaking every inch of my body.

Time passed, I know, but I didn't feel it pass. My clothes felt heavy, my legs weighted, as I treaded through the muddy landscape. My eyes burned, and nothing appeared clear anymore. My body was giving in. I had put up a good fight, but I couldn't run from this. I couldn't stop this. I slowly crumbled into the soggy earth and began to cry.

The soft, wet earth embraced my body while my mind spun with thoughts I didn't understand. Over the last few years, I had learned to cope with many things—the numerous rumors concerning my move to Red River Parish, the emptiness of not knowing my past, who I was, or what had become of my family—but not this. I had never confided in anyone the way I had with Erik—never allowed myself to be this vulnerable. And here I was exposed, defenseless to the pain.

Lifting myself from the mush, I purposed to forget Erik—to forget I ever called him my friend. I could be strong, I told myself. But I knew I was lying.

-2-

THREAT

OUR HOUSE LOOKED DARK AND UNWELCOMING IN THE downpour. Pools of rain always collected on the roof before dripping down the white shutters. The house looked like it was weeping. Appropriate, I thought.

I stepped carefully up the slippery steps of the porch—one, two, three, four. I always had to count them—one of my idiosyncrasies. With my remaining energy, I raked off my sneakers and reached for the door.

The familiar cluttered walls welcomed me home. I dragged myself upstairs, past the crooked paintings that Alice had recently hung, sliding my hand along the rail. Twelve steps to the top, six steps into my room, and eight more into my bathroom. I made it to the bathroom sink in ten steps.

Staring back from the mirror was a face I hardly recognized. My eyes were swollen and pink from the tears—my hair a knotted mess. Traces of splattered mud speckled my face and neck, while the remainder of it caked my clothes. I was exhausted from it all—the running, the crying, the deception. And for the first time, I could see the damage.

I stumbled over to the old claw-foot tub, still dewy from my morning shower, and twisted the hot water nozzle to the shower on—all the way on. I shifted out of my jacket, then stepped into the tub wearing the rest of my muck-covered clothes and pulled the plastic lining, until I was sealed in with a cloud of steam.

The heat and the pressure from the water calmed my nerves as it washed away the brush and grime from my skin and clothes. Before long my jeans were clean enough to take off, then my shirt. I closed my eyes and sank to the back of the tub, listening only to the hissing of the water. My mind was almost at ease.

"You normally shower with clothes on?"

Erik. One hand quickly shot over my chest to cover my bra, and the other one to my underwear.

"What are you doing here? Get out!" No one had ever seen that much of my skin before—I felt my face turn red.

"No."

"No?" I waited, fuming with detest.

"That's right. I'm not going anywhere—but you can try to run again." He chuckled. He seemed to be enjoying the situation. He looped his fingers around a red towel hanging on the wall. It moved back and forth on its hook, taunting me.

"Give me the towel."

"No." Our eyes met. "We're going to talk first," he said.

"You think this is funny, don't you?" I pulled my knees up and curled my arms around them to hide my exposed skin. I still felt mortified that he was seeing me this way. "This is nothing but a game to you."

Erik pulled at his soaked T-shirt, loosening the gray material from the hard lines of his abdomen, and then tossed the towel over his shoulder. There was no doubting his beauty and my attraction to him.

"I find it entertaining, yes. But this isn't a game." With a devilish grin, he trotted forward to the tub and turned the water off. "I was very surprised with your reaction today. I didn't think you had it in you."

I didn't say anything. I couldn't think of a clear way to address what was just said, and in all honesty, I agreed with him. When have I ever stood up to anyone?

"Something big is about to happen, Clara. And it will be easier if we are friends."

"I don't want anything to do with you," I blurted.

"You're only making this process harder on yourself." In one smooth motion, he lowered himself, balancing his weight on the edge of the porcelain tub. "You will eventually have to let go, or there will be much to endure."

He was telling me what to do again, and I didn't like it.

I quickly grabbed a handful of his shirt and pulled with all my weight. He toppled over the edge of the tub, while I jumped out with the red towel in hand. I sprinted through the bathroom door and slid into my room, but before I could slam the door behind me, his arms closed around my shoulders.

"Let go of me!" My voice came out like a growl.

"Stop fighting me, doll."

Doll. His voice. His touch. My knees went weak. He loosened an arm to rest it against my collarbone and then moved his hand over my skin. I couldn't speak. I felt his cold fingertips follow the freckles on my shoulder to my neck. It was a gentle touch, barely making contact with my skin, but it had a chilling effect.

Chill bumps formed on my arms as he pressed the palm of his hand in the crease of my neck. I could hear his breath quicken behind me. His scent, the scent of peppermint, filled the air as his fingers moved to trace the contours of my cheek. He carefully tilted my head so that our eyes met—I was trapped somewhere in his dark gaze.

"We are not like the people in this parish. You and I, we are different. We come from another place."

Different. I had heard that word before.

"Clara." His voice was soft and low, flowing through the air like a distant song. "I know about the dreams. I know you are afraid of them. Don't be, Clara. He calls for you. Give him control—let him in."

He leaned down so that his cheek rested against mine. His silky hair brushed against my face. I could smell the woods in his hair—I could feel the warmth in his sweet breath. Everything stopped. I could no longer hear the rain beat down on the roof or the branches of the ancient cypress tree scrape against my bedroom window. The load roar of the old air-conditioning unit seemed to whisper now, and I was no longer breathing. His words had taken a hold of me.

"I'll take you to him when the time is right." He sandwiched my face between his hand and cheek. "Don't try to run. We will find you."

I couldn't speak for what felt like hours, but in reality was only seconds. My mind was whirling around like a tornado had landed. I could only focus on the words he fed me. *Let him in.*

And then I felt a part of my mind fight back. Like an opposing magnet—pushing his words away. A spark of some sort.

I felt his grip loosen as he slowly shuffled back from me. Even though I despised him, I wasn't ready for him to let go.

Darkness had already filled my room when my mind came soaring back to me. I was standing alone, staring blankly at the shadows in the window. My towel was still loosely wrapped around me, my hair still slightly damp. I'm not sure how long I had been standing there alone. I'm not sure when he had left me or why.

I wanted nothing more than to crawl into bed and disappear amongst the blue and brown waves of sheets. I sat down on the edge of its lumpy surface and looked back.

I spent the rest of the gloomy night in that one lumpy spot, rolled in the red towel that once teased me. My stare stayed fixated on the crooked branches that waved outside my window, until the limbs were completely swallowed by the night.

Throughout the evening, the air conditioner kicked on and off, blasting gusts of piercing cold air through my room. My hair turned to a cold mass of curls. I shivered, but had no desire to move. The cold felt right. I hoped that the thoughts Erik left me with would go away, but as the hours rolled by, they remained stuck in my head. Every word. Every look. Every touch. Stuck. And no matter how hard I tried to push them away, my mind kept coming back to one thing. *We will find you.*

I couldn't sleep. Every time my eyelids closed, I replayed the entire day. It was like watching a poorly written movie. It kept replaying and rewinding. My mind chose to create alternate endings—things I could have said, should have said to him. Before long, I was romanticizing about the very person I thought I hated.

Erik's look had never been an innocent one; it always implied an undeniable desire, a longing for something unobtainable, and an unfaltering passion. His look had been even more convincing tonight. That look said it all. I wanted to know how his lips felt. I wanted to know if the chilling electricity that flowed from his touch would tingle from his lips. My heart jumped erratically. I didn't *mean* to have these thoughts. I didn't *want* to have these thoughts. They simply appeared in my mind, like any other idea or feeling.

I let my eyes wander around my dark bedroom, hoping that something would catch my attention long enough to push all the uncomfortable feelings aside. The moonlight splintered through my window and softly touched the posters of Paris, Ireland, and Hawaii. They were all places I had hoped to run away to. My dresser sat against the decorated walls, organized as always, everything dusted and positioned forward in a straight line. It wasn't much to look at, but everything there was significant to me.

The line began with a framed picture of my Aunt Alice—a picture I had taken last year while she was blowing out her birthday candles. She had a smile stretched from ear to ear; it was my favorite picture of her. Stacks of journals and figurines sat next to the frame, all gifts from an old friend. The line ended with a small leather bible—my mother's childhood bible. It had been my homecoming gift from Alice. Many nights had I pored over the pages, reading every printed word carefully and tracing over the notes my mom had once scribbled in the margin. What little peace I possessed came from that book. It was all that remained from my forgotten past.

An uncontrollable shiver came over me. I thought back to the moment Erik's palm lay against my skin. The surge of energy from his touch had felt like fire running through my veins. It had warmed my skin and heated the entire room. As much as I despised him, I was attracted to him. I knew it was wrong, but I wanted him to hold me again.

The knot in my stomach tightened, sending a warning to my brain. My emotions were battling the thin protective barrier of sound reasoning. I needed a diversion. It was time for a midnight snack.

Alice was downstairs eating a bowl of warmed-up potato stew and reading yesterday's newspaper. Her dirty blonde hair was pulled back loosely in a rubber band, leaving only a few strands to frame her heart-shaped face. My aunt was a nurse at the Coushatta Health Care Center, so midnight stew was a part of her nightly routine.

Unfortunately I looked nothing like my aunt. She had bold, almond-shaped eyes that were always a bright shade of sea blue. Her sun-kissed skin was flawless under any light—including the unforgiving fluorescents in our kitchen. She was a few inches shorter than me, but she had a body that grabbed the attention of every man she came in contact with in the entire parish. She was only a few years shy of forty, and she never tried to be beautiful—she just was. Naturally.

I cleared my throat as I scooted a kitchen chair away from the round edge of the table. "I didn't hear you come in—been home long?"

Her pink lips curled up with a spoon still dangling from her mouth. "Just long enough to nuke the stew and catch up on some news." Her eyes continued to skim the paper. "You didn't tell me Fergus took over Swamp Tours. He didn't leave the library, did he?"

Fergus was the town's old, quirky librarian, but to us, he was a dear family friend—a grandfather figure. He had all but confirmed this role by celebrating every birthday, every holiday, and every special occasion with us. And every time I went to the library for one of his notorious book readings, he always made excuses to give me things. Journals. Crosses. Figurines. Thanks to him I had quite the collection on my dresser, but I liked it—I imagined that's how a grandfather would be.

"Oh. I thought you knew. It was last week, I believe. Fergus bought Swamp Tours—boats and all—from old Marcel," I said.

Her eyes narrowed.

"Why are you giving me that look?"

"He never mentioned he was interested in the tourism business." She took another heaping spoonful of stew before continuing. "And I can't believe Marcel sold out after all of these years."

"Well, Marcel's been complaining about business being slow for a while now. The last few weeks I've only had twelve hours scheduled—and I'm one of the lucky ones. Jean's doing good to get one shift, and it's usually Saturday, so she tries to trade it off," I said.

"Huh. Seems I've fallen behind. Any other news I've missed?"

"You probably won't see Erik around here anytime soon." I had planned on keeping this news to myself, simply because my aunt really liked Erik, but the information slipped out before I could stop it.

"Oh, honey…what happened?"

"It's pretty stupid," I said. "I don't feel up to talking about it yet. I just thought you should know that I won't be riding to school with him anymore."

"Well," she said, "don't you dare feel stupid about something like that. My momma used to say, 'You ain't the first to feel this way, and you certainly ain't the last, so never let it get you down.'"

Alice smiled, taking in a moment from her distant memories. That's one of the many things I loved about her—she was full of quotes.

"Things will be back to normal before you know it, hon."

"Thanks." I decided it would be a good idea to leave the conversation at that. "So—you think you might have some time off from the hospital this weekend?"

"Sorry, toots. They have me down for the evening shift all weekend," she said as she scraped the last bit of stew from her bowl. "But, I'll be home tomorrow night. I was hoping to make dinner for us. Figure you could use a break from those microwaveable dinners." She carefully backed away from the table with her empty bowl and glass in hand and then softly placed them in the sink.

"That would be great, actually."

"Perfect. I hate to leave good company, but I better get in bed. I've got to be back at work in about six hours. Don't forget about our dinner date tomorrow, okay?"

"I won't," I replied. And with a swift hug, Alice made her way upstairs to her bedroom.

I heated a small mug of milk in the microwave and then trotted with it up the stairs. The sheets on my bed had already cooled when I rolled back into them, making the warm milk feel and even taste better rolling down my throat. I stared into the darkness of my room, sipping on the mug until all of the milk was gone, and then leaned back into my pillow to stare some more. I wasn't sure what time it was when I finally drifted asleep—I just know that I did, because I fell into the dream that scared me the most.

Walls crumbled all around me. An undeniable force pulled at my core. I tried to fight it, I tried to deny it the power, but I was weak. I felt pain in my side, and I knew that this dark force was winning. My veins started to burn, and I screamed, but it didn't stop. I was alone, but I didn't feel alone. I could still hear his voice.

"Clara, Clara. Stay with me, Clara." His voice embraced me even in death. He was part of me somehow, this nameless, faceless angel. His voice had flooded my soul, comforting me like a perfect song through the pain.

I screamed for him. *"Angel!"*

He never heard me. I soared through a tunnel. A pale light became incredibly bright, taking all my pain and fear as it surrounded me. Then there was nothing. I loved him—that was my torment.

-3-

RRPH

THAT MORNING I WOKE UP AN HOUR EARLY TO CALL JEANNA Beaudet. Jeanna, who everyone called Jean for short, was voted friendliest girl two years in a row at school. Jean was the first person to talk to me mid-freshman year on my dreaded first day of high school, and we became fast friends after we managed to snag the same weekend job as tour guides for Swamp Tours.

The phone rang once, twice, three times, and then on the fourth ring, I heard the phone tumble off the hook.

"Hello?" Her voice was low and scratchy; I could tell that I'd woken her.

"Hey, can I get a ride this morning?"

The phone picked up the sound of sheets rustling. "Where's Erik? Everyone knows you ride with him." The question was barely audible, but clear enough to make my stomach twist.

"Yeah, well, he can't take me today. Do you think you could swing by? I could meet you at the end of the road."

Jean had just gotten a shiny red MINI Cooper for her birthday. It was a nice car with a lot of pep, but the dirt road that wound to my house was spotted with dozens of deep potholes that stayed filled with muddy water. And since it had been raining for days,

I knew that she would never agree to pick me up if she had to force her car down that road.

"All right, if you meet me at the end of the road. I'll be out there in a little over an hour. You owe me, though—say, this Saturday, shift trade?"

"Umm, yeah, that's fine."

"Perfect. See ya in a little, Clara Bear."

"See ya."

Click.

I took a very long shower. I stayed under the hot, steady flow of water, until it began to turn cold. My fingers and toes had become prune-like from the overhydration, but every second in the shower relaxed my tense muscles. My whole body felt tight—uncomfortable, from my lack of sleep that night. I wasn't ready to face the world—a world filled with noisy, spiteful classmates who would be prying for new gossip. News traveled fast in our town, and since Erik and I had both missed school yesterday, a red flag would already be up—probably waving on the silver flagpole in the courtyard of our school. Not literally, but it might as well be there.

All I wanted to do was crawl back into bed, pull the covers over my face, and then go into hibernation. Too bad that wasn't an option.

I stepped out of the shower to towel-dry my hair. Wet curls cascaded down from my head and fell against my back. Even my hair felt heavier than usual. The mirror reflected the same sad stranger from yesterday. Same puffy eyes, same dull skin—just free of mud this time.

I grabbed a powder compact from the small plastic basket of beauty supplies on my marbled vanity. I swirled a sponge into the compact and then applied the ivory powder to my skin, making sure to double-coat the areas around my eyes. The dark purple circles eventually faded, but the powder didn't camouflage my swollen lids. I grabbed a small brush and the lightest shimmery eye shadow I owned and then dabbed the light-reflecting pigment into the corners of my eyes. It was a trick Jean had taught me—a trick to brighten tired eyes. It seemed to help. After a couple coats of mascara, I noticed I didn't look half bad.

The walk to my closet was a chilly one, but it only took a minute to find clothes that would work—a casual purple dress with plain black tights. When I first moved to Coushatta, the weather had stayed sunny and bright, with an occasional evening shower or thunderstorm. But in the last few months, there had been a noticeable increase in rain. My wardrobe was proof of that change.

I trotted downstairs with a bag full of books to my side. I had plenty of time for breakfast. I never was big on eating in the morning—I liked breakfast food, just not a fan of eating that early in the day. But since I had skipped eating altogether yesterday, my stomach was insisting that breakfast was a good idea. Particularly, toast and bacon sounded good.

I dug around in the refrigerator until I found my aunt's turkey bacon. I grabbed the bacon, butter, and a jar of grape jam from the fridge, and then the loaf of wheat bread that was rolled up on the counter. In minutes I had the two slices of bread buttered and toasted—with a few slices of bacon sizzling in the microwave.

Ding. Breakfast was served.

I cleaned and stored the dishes before locking up the house. I had ample time to walk down the curvy road to meet with Jean—could have stayed in the house another half hour actually, but I felt like I had to get out. There was nothing else I could do in there to keep my mind off of him or the dreaded day ahead of me. I had to keep moving. At least, that was the only thing I knew I could do.

The dirt road appeared hidden in the haze of the morning. Dew still glistened on the ferns that separated the road from the woods, while rain puddles attempted to soak into the damp green earth. I dodged muddy potholes and tuned in to the sound of the tree frogs singing to the crickets. I caught a small breeze in my hair as I turned the corner of the first curve in the road. The strong fragrance of wet pine hit me like a ton of bricks. Even the woodsy smell reminded me of Erik.

Jean was grinning with a mouthful of food as soon as I opened the car door. Her white teeth shined against her creamy brown skin like a Cheshire cat. She had obviously had a good start to her morning—at least she had a good breakfast from what I could see. The smell of hot caramel coffee filled the small car, and a few crumbs of coffee cake remained on her shirt. She was still chewing when she spoke.

"Mornin', sunshine!" A few more crumbs fell to her shirt. If it were anyone else talking with a hunk of cake stuffing her mouth, it might seem disgusting, but with Jean, it was almost cute.

"Hey, thanks for picking me up. How's the cake?" I forced a quick grin while closing the door behind me.

"Delicious," she said. I watched as more crumbs flew in the air. She chewed for a few seconds before quickly swallowing what was left of her breakfast. "But I didn't pick you up to talk about cake." She shifted the car into drive, eased onto the highway, and then slowly accelerated toward the Coushatta city limits sign. "You gonna tell me what's going on between you and Erik—or do I need to interrogate you?"

"Ummm..." The sound came from my lips before I had even realized my lips were parted. I turned to the window, looking to the trees as if they might save me from the conversation. But nothing happened.

"He really got to you, didn't he?"

I felt awkward thinking about the question.

He had gotten to me—that was the problem. He had managed to gain my trust, and then he threw me to the wolves. Even though Jean knew the answer, I wasn't ready to say it out loud. I looked over to her and could see the sincerity in her eyes. I supposed my face said it all.

"What a jerk—don't you worry about him, Clara. Not one bit. He's not worth your time." Her dark, curly hair bounced while she shook her head. "Besides, he always looks like he's on something. I bet he's a pothead." She kept talking as if she were trying to solve a mystery. "Yeah, that would explain it all.

His dilated pupils, his weird behaviors. He's always wearing those stupid dark sunglasses, and—and—that would definitely explain why he hurt you. I hear drugs make you irrational or crazy or something."

Even though her speech had been off the wall, there was a bit of truth behind it. He did wear sunglasses, every day—even when it was overcast. His pupils were dilated every time his glasses were off, which wasn't very often. He did have strange and unusual behavior. And last night, he didn't make a lick of sense. Could it be drugs? Maybe he did smoke pot. Surely I would have noticed something as obvious as that.

"No, I don't think that's it. He's not that type."

"Well, you never know. You need to stop putting him on a pedestal, girl. He's only human—a hot human, but still just human. And there are plenty more where that came from." She said this with such assurance that I almost nodded in agreement.

The rest of the drive was filled with Jean making random statements about Erik and other boys at our school—trying to make me feel better. In some sense it helped, but it kept my mind on the night before. By the time we had made it to the school parking lot, she had reminded me of all the bad breakups and relationships in our school. She ventured off a few times, referring to relationship issues in movies like *Ten Things I Hate About You* and *When Harry Met Sally*. She had a knack for relating real life to chick flicks—another quality I loved about her.

She made a few more attempts to extract information from me as we walked down the halls to class. I never budged.

"You know I'm nosy. I'm gonna wonder what happened all day—and we know I'll eventually get it out of you. So"—she paused for dramatic effect—"you should tell me now. That way we both feel better."

"Bye, Jean."

"Fine. I'll see ya at lunch. And don't you try to skip out on me. I know all your hiding spots," she said with a cheesy smile.

"Okay, see ya."

Every eye in RRHS was glued to me in class.

Aside from the initial shock from Erik hanging around me, this was the most attention I had ever gotten at school. I could hear Erik's name brought up in the wispy conversations from the back of my chemistry class, followed by my name and a quick glance from the clones.

I heard laughter erupt from the back of the room, and I looked over my shoulder to catch a glimpse of Lydia. Lydia was the girl who everyone wanted to be seen with at our school. To adults, she seemed innocent enough—always smiling, answering politely with *yes, ma'am* and *no, ma'am*, turning homework in on time—but to any student who didn't idolize her, she was a vicious, rumor-spreading witch.

On the back row, Lydia's long legs were stretched in the aisle so that they were accessible for every guy in the room to view—including Mr. Buckster, our perverted chemistry teacher. Every guy seemed to be taking advantage of the open viewing. Today, her long bleach-blonde hair was pulled back in a high ponytail with a maroon ribbon that matched her short cheerleading uniform. Even in a quick glance I could see her lashes flutter and her smile widen as she whispered to Rachel, her brunette clone. I could only imagine what rumors they were already spreading.

I had readied myself for the whispers and the nosy questions—the strange looks and the possible rumors. I maintained a calm and relaxed composure all throughout chemistry and Spanish. I even managed to force a fake smile or two along the way. But there was one thing I hadn't expected. One thing I couldn't have prepared for.

It happened at lunch.

I went to lunch as usual, but the cafeteria was colder than usual—whiter than usual. Eyes watched me enter the cafeteria and followed me through the lunch line. They were the eyes of a group of girls sitting near the salad bar, a group I recognized. The *posh* group. The *better than thou* group. The stuck-ups. The clones. And their queen, Lydia, and her sidekick, Rachel, sat in the middle of them.

Usually these girls never gave me the time of day—never acted as if I existed, unless I was in their way. One time Lydia and I were actually assigned as lab partners—she never spoke a word, never acknowledged I was speaking to her or even alive. She simply kept her nose held high and then seductively whispered something in Mr. Buckster's ear. Whatever she said landed me a big fat F and her—well, she got a new lab partner. I didn't like her much after that. Her clone followers were no different.

As I scooted across the cafeteria to my usual table, the corner table furthest from the food lines and trash cans, I felt their beady eyes following me. The uncomfortable feeling was quickly interrupted with a startling jolt from Jean.

"What took ya so long? Luke and I went ahead and split a pizza. He had to go retake a pre-cal quiz, and I couldn't wait any longer. I was starvin'. Gym was such a beatin' today—really worked up my appetite."

Luke Dubois was Jean's new boyfriend. They actually made a cute couple. Luke was what I liked to call all-American. He was around six foot, blond hair, blue eyes, muscular, and the best linebacker on our football team. Though I was quite fond of the guy—he was polite, laughed a lot, and he really seemed to care about Jean—I was relieved to hear he wouldn't be joining us for lunch. Now that Erik and I wouldn't be sitting together, I would be the awkward third wheel.

"I was caught up in class. You know, finishing up some work," I lied. The truth was I hadn't realized that I was almost fifteen minutes late to lunch. My time was not matching up with the time in the real world. I probably wouldn't have noticed if she hadn't pointed it out.

"Well, hurry up. Sit down. Eat your salad."

"That's my plan," I said.

Jean started rambling as soon as I sat my tray down. "Girl, let me tell ya—I followed my pizza with one of these delicious milk chocolate toffee with almonds candies. I thought I would treat myself after the day I've been havin'. We actually had to play scooter board softball in gym today. Who comes up with this stuff?"

Before I could answer, she had already gone to the next subject.

"And you know that game where you stand in a circle and throw from the free throw? Remember when we played that last year?" She paused just long enough for me to nod my head before she continued, "Well, we had to play that after the scooter board softball, and I lost…again. I tell ya what, you are so lucky that you don't have to take it this year. I think PE should be banned altogether. It only reminds me that I lack coordination." She opened her purse to pull out another wrapped candy. "I always leave feelin' bad."

"At least you didn't flunk your Spanish test today. Got any candy for that?"

"What? I thought you said you were prepared." Jean slid a couple of gold-wrapped candies onto the table. "Here. You'll be surprised how the chocolate helps."

"I was prepared," I said. I rolled up the left sleeve of my jacket to reveal a jumble of black, smudged letters on my skin.

"Really, Clara? No one gets away with cheating in Maywert's class."

"I know that now," I mumbled.

"Since when do you cheat anyway?"

"I was going to study, but then everything happened…I couldn't think after that."

"Have you bumped into him today?"

"Nu-uh."

"That's probably a good thing. You don't want to deal with that anywhere on school grounds. If you or Erik caused a scene—that would be gossip for months. Anyway, I've been thinkin' about this whole situation between the two of you, and I think I figured it out." Jean scooted her orange plastic chair closer to mine, giving me just enough time to swallow a mouthful of lettuce. "Y'all did it, didn't you?"

"Excuse me?" I was shocked by her bluntness. "Of course not."

"Why are you holding out on me? You can tell me—I won't repeat a word, honest I won't. Everything's not black-and-white these days. There's a lot of gray area. I won't judge you. I like to go by the first, second, and third base rules. That's what happened, isn't it? He broke your rules—he went too far?"

"No, that's not it. We've never even kissed," I timidly replied. I felt embarrassed as soon as the words left my lips. I imagined I was the only girl in the entire parish who hadn't been kissed. I quickly broke eye contact by turning my attention to my plastic fork picking through the colorful salad in front of me and then continued, "I'm not sure I've ever been kissed."

"Really? So you really don't know? I always wondered about that. I thought the memory loss thing was just another one of the poshes' attempts at a nasty rumor, but jeez—that's bad."

"Thanks." I grabbed my salad bowl and empty Dasani bottle while I pushed my chair away from the table, but before I could stand, her hand caught my sleeve.

"Come on. You know I always speak before I think. I didn't mean to upset you. You just surprised me. I mean, you never tell me anything personal. And—well, that's big." She released her grip on my sleeve to softly pat me on the shoulder. "I want you to know that I'm here for you. And I'll stop buggin' ya about Erik."

I stared into the crowd of students shoveling food into their mouths, trying to eat the last bit of cafeteria slop before the bell sounded. I knew Jean would never hurt me on purpose. I trusted her—I wanted to tell her everything, but as I looked back to meet her concerned eyes, the bell rang. It was an annoyingly long bell. Good timing, I supposed.

"Thank you for being such a good friend. We'll talk on the way home. Okay?" I said with a genuine smile.

"Yeah?" Her face twisted, surprised that I had caved in.

"Yeah. I'll tell you anything you want to know."

"I swear—you just made my day! I promise you won't regret it." She shot a quick glance to the large clock displayed on the cafeteria wall. "I better haul butt if I'm going to make algebra on time. I can't afford another tardy. Will ya meet me in the parking lot after school?"

"Gotcha, I'll be there."

"I can't wait! Later tater!"

I should have gotten up right then. I should have chucked the rest of my grazed salad and bee-lined out of the cafeteria to my third-period class. But I didn't. I sat there picking at the carrots hidden in my bowl of lettuce, zoned out. The tables were clearing out with each minute past the bell, but I didn't move. It wasn't until I heard my name that I noticed Queen Posh and her jester walking toward my table.

"Hello, Clara. Are you enjoying your lunch?" Lydia asked.

Crap. Too late to hide.

In the two and a half years I'd been at RRPH, the posh girls had never spoken a word to me. Now, today of all days, the queen of all the evil girls decided to ask about my lunch? *You've got to be kidding me.*

I plastered a fake smile on my face and answered sarcastically, "Couldn't be better."

Next thing I knew, Lydia and Rachel plopped down in the chairs beside me. I was now the middle filling of a posh sandwich.

"So I heard you and Erik aren't talking anymore. That sucks," Lydia said.

"That really sucks," Rachel agreed.

"I'm sure you're real torn up about it," I shot back.

"Well, it was only a matter of time. I mean, it didn't make sense, you and Erik."

"Oh, but you and Erik do," I said sarcastically. I could see exactly where this was going. I was upset to even think such a thing, much alone say it, but I managed to keep a strong tone.

"Exactly. *Everyone* knows that. Every guy at this school wants to be with me. It's a fact," she said.

Rachel chimed in, "Yeah. Lydia is hot. And you—well, you're no Lydia."

Okay, they were really ticking me off. It was no secret that Lydia had a thing for Erik. She had been drooling over him since his first day at school. Surprisingly, Erik never seemed the slightest bit interested in her big boobs, her perfectly bronzed skin, or her long legs, but it still bothered me that she implied he would be.

"What do you want, Lydia?"

"You sure don't beat around the bush. I like that." She slowly leaned forward and crossed her arms on the top of the table. "I want his number. You won't be needing it anymore, so why not give it to someone who can use it?" Her eyelashes fluttered, while her glossed lips turned up into a devilish smirk.

The thought of her calling Erik was worse than the idea that I might never call him again. I immediately felt nauseous. "You're not his type," I replied through gritted teeth.

"But I am," she said smugly. "It won't be long before he calls me. I simply want to beat him to the punch."

"That's ridiculous. I'm not giving you anything." I forcefully pushed my chair away from the table—away from the evil queen. "Just leave me alone."

"If that's how you want to be"—Lydia threw a folded piece of notebook paper on the table as she stood from her chair—"you can see for yourself. I was trying to save you from the harsh truth." She dramatically flipped her hair, signaling her clone it was time to leave. "And Clara, when you get over the obvious fact that he doesn't want you, you can leave his number in my locker. Locker three-five-one. Thanks."

I hated her uneven locker number almost as much as I hated her. Lydia left with her cold signature smirk across her face. I left with a folded note addressed from Erik to her.

English was an uncomfortable event. I sat the folded letter on my desk and stared at it until my overweight English teacher threatened to take it up. Apparently, the tragedy of Macbeth was much more important than my own personal tragedy. The bell rang after a painful hour and a half, saving me from the embarrassing task of reading the part of Lady Macbeth to the class. I was out the door in a flash. Good timing, yet again.

I charged through the entrance of my history class, took my usual seat in the back of the room, and frantically unfolded the note.

Lydia,
We need to talk. She knows. Meet me tomorrow, the usual time and place.
-Erik

Those words pierced through my chest like a long, crooked blade and ached from within. The betrayal was far worse and went much deeper than I had imagined possible. Shakespeare couldn't have written a better tragedy. Feeling like my heart had been sliced in two, I crumbled the note and slumped down in my desk.

I raised my head once class had officially started, but my mind was not there. It was far, far away in an unhappy place. Lydia had told the truth. Erik never wanted me. I was a fool to think he ever did. I couldn't wait for this day to be over.

3:15 p.m.. I had made it through the day. I was beaten. I was broken. But I had made it through alive. Jean was sitting in her car, anxiously awaiting the talk I had promised her. I was met with an enthusiastic smile as soon as I opened the car door.

I wasn't sure what needed to be said to explain my past. It was a touchy subject for me, one that was difficult for me to explain to myself.

It was clear that Jean was holding back, trying to avoid her bad habit of asking questions and speaking without thinking.

"You don't have to do this—if you changed your mind, I totally understand."

I sighed. "No, I want to. I'm trying to think of where to begin."

"Just start from the beginnin'. Like, where are you from, and what's the whole deal with your memory loss? You never would tell me."

"Right. Okay. I'm not entirely sure how to answer that. I only know what I've been told by Alice."

"Well, what did she tell you?"

"That my mom's family, the Leblancs, they were born and raised here, in Louisiana. That's why my aunt kept me here."

"So your aunt is your mom's sister?"

"Yeah. Alice was my mom's baby sister. Alice Leblanc. My mom's name was Marie. Well, their parents—my grandparents—died when they were both pretty young. It was a car wreck, I think. Alice moved to Coushatta shortly after that, and my mom left for Ireland."

"Ireland? That's awesome," Jean said.

"Well, my mom fell in love with an Irishman, Brogan Calahan—my dad. So she stayed in Ireland with him and his family. They married, had me, and…well, that's really all we know. The rest is kind of sketchy." I paused long enough to push the hair out of my face, tucking it behind my ears. "Apparently we moved around a lot. From what Alice says, we spent most of our time in Ireland, but we came to Coushatta a few times. She said that we were planning on visiting her again, but never showed up. There was some kind of accident."

She was quiet for a moment, readily waiting for me to continue. "Is that why you have trouble remembering your past—because of this accident?"

"We think so," I muttered in response.

"You don't remember anything?"

"Nothing at all. No memories. No faces. No images. I just woke up in the hospital in Coushatta, feeling like my head was going to split open. I didn't know where I was—who I was. Alice was the first person I saw, and I had no memory of even knowing her."

"That had to be hard—waking up to a world you didn't know."

"It was hard for me to take in. I was angry at the world for a long time, even at Alice." We both sat quietly in the car for a few minutes, Jean focusing on the sparse traffic that was on the road while my eyes darted from one road sign to the next.

"So what happened to your folks?"

"Don't know. Alice flew to Ireland, but she didn't know where to look. She said my mom would never tell her where we lived. That it was safer that way."

"Oh my goodness," she said. "I'm so sorry. I wish you would have told me sooner so I could have been there for you."

"You were there for me when I needed you, Jean. I should have told you instead of Erik."

"What happened with him?"

"Well..." I hesitated for a moment, collecting my thoughts. "I like to write in a journal. It's kind of my way of coping with everything. I write my thoughts down, my dreams. I describe images that I remember, and then I try to link them together."

"What did he do?" Jean asked as if she already knew.

"I found one of the pages in his jacket pocket. Apparently, he's been going through my things—stealing my entries."

"Oh. My. Gosh." Jean pulled off the highway and parked in her usual spot on the dirt road. "What did he say?"

"It's hard to say—I think he threatened me."

"What did Alice say about all of this?" Jean looked more and more worried with each question.

"I haven't told her," I said.

"What? Jeez, then promise me you'll tell her."

I sighed for a second, thinking about the reaction she would have after I explained to her that I was threatened. I knew that I should have told her about it, but I had hoped to avoid it altogether. Alice already had too much on her plate to worry about.

"Promise me," Jean insisted again.

I shifted in my seat to unlock my seat belt—a little hint that I was ready to leave.

"All right. I'll tell her." I stepped out of the car. "Can I get a ride tomorrow morning?"

"Sure thing. I'll be here. Just make sure you talk to your aunt."

I gave her a smile and closed the door, mouthing good-bye from outside the passenger window.

-4-

UNUSUAL

ALICE WAS PLACING TWO BOWLS OF HER FAMOUS FOUR-HOUR gumbo on the table when I walked through the door. The house was filled with a seafood smell mixed with the spicy scent of simmering onions, celery, and bell pepper. You could almost taste the gumbo by sniffing the air.

Any other day I would have been excited about spending time with my aunt. I would have been excited about eating gumbo and catching up on the town's scandalous gossip, possibly sharing a few laughs over the pecan pie—but tonight I was hoping to find a way out of talking. Hoping to share a meal in silence.

Aside from the usual hello, we went through the motions of setting the rest of the table without speaking. From what I could tell, something was weighing on Alice's mind as much or more than what was on my own.

We finally sat down to eat. We talked about the weather mostly. Alice did ask a few more questions about Fergus and the Swamp Tour business—I asked about the hospital and when her next day off might be. That was pretty much it. It was a dinner filled with small talk. We finished the main course, and to my surprise, Alice still had not asked about Erik or school.

It was during dessert that things got awkward.

I had just swallowed my first bite of pie when Alice said something that completely caught me off guard.

"Anything unusual happen to you in the last few days?" She asked as if it were an assumption, as if she already knew the answer and was waiting for me to explain.

Unusual? It was an odd question, one that was very hard to answer considering the recent events that had transpired with Erik. That was unusual, indeed, but hardly something to pique an adult's interest. And how did she even know? I had only told Jean, not even an hour ago. Guess there was no way out of telling her about Erik's warning.

Alice asked again before I had time to reply. "Anything possibly out of the ordinary?"

I told her the story from the beginning. It was modified, leaving out the fact that Erik snuck into the house while I was in the shower, but it was still a pretty accurate version of what had happened. Threat and all.

At first I was stuck on figuring out the look she gave in response to my confession. Her expression wasn't a disappointed one or an angry one. It was more of a frightened look. Surely she didn't believe we were in any kind of immediate danger.

"I should have told you sooner, but I didn't want you to worry over something like this," I admitted. "How'd you even find out?"

As if her brain was still processing everything, she replied mechanically, “I didn’t. I received a call from your school today. You cheated on your Spanish test.”

“Oh.” I had been preparing for the wrong speech. I had completely forgotten about the Spanish test.

“Erik threatened you?” Her body tensed as she spoke.

I nodded. “Yeah, but I think he was only doing it to get to me.”

I was instantly bothered by her reaction. It seemed completely out of character. She seemed on edge and not the least bit interested that I cheated in Spanish.

“How would you like to get out of town this weekend? We could leave after you get home from school. Take a road trip. What do you think?”

Her on-call cell phone, the one that sounded every time the hospital needed her to fill another shift, rang. She almost jumped out of her chair.

“I better take this upstairs—I’ll talk to them about the time off. Can you pick up the kitchen?”

“Yeah, that sounds great. I’ll clean up.” I motioned for her take the call.

Little did I know—we would never make that trip.

-5-

SHADOW

Only in Red River Parish would a public library sandwiched between an antique mall and a fried boudin stand be considered a popular destination on any given afternoon. I sighed at the very thought and slowly marched up the steps of Coushatta's historic library.

As I opened the heavy door to the library entrance, I inhaled the air that was trying hard to escape. I always enjoyed the smell that occupied the halls of the library. The smell was enchanting. Every book seemed to radiate this particular scent. It was the scent of adventure.

I walked to the very back of the library, passing all of the interesting sections, to the dreaded poetry aisle. There was a small one-person desk conveniently set up facing the wall at the end of the aisle. I almost sympathized with the desk—it sat trapped between the walls of old, forgotten poetry. At least by the end of the night, I would be escaping from this dungeon.

Now it was time to focus. I shook my head as I recalled the look of pure excitement when my English teacher announced our paper would be on our favorite poem. Any poem. Any century. I let my eyes wander up and down the dimly lit shelves, skimming the names of the greats. *Edgar Allan Poe. Langston Hughes. Charles Dickens.*

Then I noticed something unusual. A small collection of books was wedged into the corner of the bookshelf, where the side of the desk met the shelves. Underneath was a bronze nameplate with the words: *For our sweet Clara, with love.*

For our sweet Clara, with love. I immediately gave my full attention to those six words. I knelt down beside the desk and pulled out a thin leather-bound book. I smiled at my discovery as I placed it against the splintered desktop.

The book had a weathered appearance, but this didn't surprise me, considering the amount of rain Coushatta received yearly. The cover was wrapped tightly with a thin piece of leather. My fingers danced over the leather cover, until they reached the bottom right corner. My ring and index finger were now resting on what appeared to be a burned marking of the letters *CC*.

"Clara Calahan," I whispered to myself as I traced the letters with my fingers. I stared at the markings for a few moments, hearing only the slight tapping of rain rolling off the library roof.

After a few moments of hovering over the desk and gazing at this newfound treasure, I slowly sank down into the attached chair. As my back slid against the form of the chair, I began to remove the leather band from the book. After the strap was loosened, I picked up the small book and let the leather piece fall into my lap. I carefully pulled back the front cover—a beautiful sketch was revealed.

It was relaxing to gaze upon the image. The pages were a dark crème color freckled with light and dark spots—but the design was flawless. One thick line flowed down the center of the paper, while a smaller one ran horizontally to form a cross. On top of the bold cross were three interconnected triangles drawn in perfect proportion. A vine of words circled the triangles, reading: *The Father, Son, and Holy Spirit. Amen.* A Trinity. The entire design was sketched in a dark black ink, but the longer I gazed at this page, the more I doubted my initial observation. I lifted the book from the desk to catch a stray beam of light peeking through the shelves. I almost thought I saw the drawing sparkle in the light—as if the medallion was only pretending to be a drawing. I lightly touched the cross one more time before turning to the next page. On the back side of the first page, was a handwritten prayer.

> *Father, please grant me the strength to spread your light. Please give me the courage to spread truth to the darkest of lands so that every shadow may be engulfed in your light. In the name of the Father, the Son, and the Holy Spirit, amen.*

I read the prayer several times, noticing the beautiful cursive writing—the undeniable honesty behind the words. This prayer seemed very familiar to me, as if I had read it before. I unintentionally repositioned myself in the uncomfortable wooden chair while my eyes darted to the next page.

Finally be strong in the Lord and in his mighty power…

I hovered over the book, but before I could finish the sentence, the library went completely dark. I carefully helped myself out of the chair and turned around. I found myself facing pure darkness.

I reached out to the front and side of my body. I felt nothing but cold air. I carefully put one foot in front of the other, easing down the dark aisle. I had never been scared of the dark, but for some odd reason, I was on edge. Frightened. Alarmed.

On my third step, my hand hit something firm. I froze while I moved my hand up the obstacle. In a matter of seconds, something grabbed my wrist. I did not move, and I couldn't make a sound. I was telling myself to say something, but nothing could escape my lips. My heart began to beat hard and fast—trying to jump out of my chest. I tried to jerk my wrist away, but the grip became tighter. I lifted my other arm to aid in the rescue—the shadow figure grabbed it without warning. I looked up and squinted my eyes peering into what I thought was a face.

He had long, dark hair, but I couldn't see his face—only darkness. I opened my mouth to scream, but again there was no sound. An eerie feeling came over me as I felt the shadow figure leaning toward me. A thick scent of smoke and incense exuded from the man in the shadows, making it difficult to breathe. I closed my eyes and concentrated on pulling away—on breaking free. I heard a loud explosion and then opened my eyes.

-6-

LAST TRAITEUSE

I OPENED MY EYES TO FIND MYSELF TANGLED IN THE SHEETS of my small bed. Relieved that I was only having another nightmare, I rolled to my side to watch the rain beat against the window. I gazed into the belly of my room, watching the lightning flicker through my window and parade across the ceiling. The sound of rolling crackles and loud explosions followed the display of light. The storm was somewhat comforting to me now. The lightning had rescued me from a horrible dream; therefore, I was very thankful.

Since the fight with Erik, the nightmares were becoming worse. The dreams were sucking me into a world of frightening images and leaving me to wonder in confusion. It had become increasingly hard to determine what was real and what was not.

I rolled over to peek at the alarm clock; it was only a little past one, barely a new day. In an effort to avoid another nightmare, I flung the covers off and slowly rolled out of bed. It was time to talk to Erik. I hesitantly crossed my room, on a mission to call him. The pale yellow phone that was placed perfectly square on the corner of the desk seemed like a foreign object as I raised the receiver to my ear. I never enjoyed talking on the phone—tonight would be no exception. I started dialing while my eyes ventured off to my bedroom window. I had a perfect view of the house in the cemetery, his house.

419–255–373…

Before I could dial the final number, I noticed a small light oozing from the cemetery, from his house. Perfect. He couldn't sleep either. I could just go over there and confront whatever this feeling was. Better yet, I could interrogate him—find out what he knew about my past—and find out what was going on between him and Lydia.

The window in my room opened to a tiny fenced veranda. The veranda had been built close to a century ago as a sunporch for blossoming flowers and ivies, but since the cypress and willow trees now shaded that half of our house, my aunt never bothered to set out any plants. Given that the wooden patio was always empty, I simply considered that area as my reading loft on a sunny day or escape route on a sleepless night. Right now it was my escape route.

I quietly slid into an old black T-shirt, faded shorts, and my red rain boots and then unlocked the latch of the window. It was the same outfit I was wearing the night I had met Erik. As I pushed the weighted windowpane up, warm rain immediately began to pool on the inside ledge. I wasn't excited about getting wet and muddy again, but I had to talk to him. I couldn't wait any longer.

By the time I crawled through the opening and slid the window down, my hair and clothes were plastered against my skin. The raindrops were the size of nickels and were flying horizontally in the night air. I looked up, and between twisted branches I made out the faint glow of the moon covered in black clouds. This was going to be a nasty storm, but that didn't matter. I had to do this, and I had to do it now.

I stepped to the edge of the patio and wrapped my fingers around the largest branch on the tree. The wind continued to rip at the branches and moss as I descended down the belly of the old cypress. I had made this climb many times before with no problem, and I usually made the climb with a heavy bag filled with charcoal and paper, but tonight the limbs and bark of the tree fought against me.

I jumped to the ground as soon as I was close enough to land softly without hitting the parked Coupe. A spear of lightning pierced the black sky, and with its blue streak of light, I saw the scratches the tree left behind on my skin. Hopefully I wouldn't run into Alice in the morning. She would have a cow if she knew I had been out tonight. Thunder rolled from the heavens; then another jagged spear of lightning ripped the darkness.

I sprinted across the soggy field and didn't stop until I had reached the wall of the graveyard. I was strangely calm once I toppled over the crumbled ruins of the stone fence. Most people my age would have probably been scared out of their wits. Tonight the cemetery looked like it came straight out of a Stephen King novel. A canopy of trees protected the graves from the harsh flow of rain, but a light blanket of fog had swept in to take its place. The cracks of thunder seemed to echo under the trees, and the constant flash of lightning animated the figurine headstones. For the first time, it looked like a dark place.

I wondered what I would say once I saw Erik. *Should I throw my arms around him and apologize for being irrational? Should I kiss him?* I really just wanted him to hold me again and to tell me that it was all one big horrible joke. Or maybe I wanted it to be real. My mind flipped from one scenario to the other. If everything he said was true, if he had the answers to my missing past, then I had to see him. I had to know the rest of the story.

I stopped in front of the dark porch of the house in the cemetery. The fog had covered the entire entrance to the house, leaving only the two small windows under the porch visible. The flicker of light that I'd seen from my bedroom window still danced from inside the house. I inched forward and carefully felt for the two large steps that met with the wooden deck. I had never been this close to the house. For some strange reason, I had never had a desire to see inside, and once Erik and his father moved in, he insisted that we keep our distance, that his father liked his privacy. The wood creaked below my feet. I was beginning to feel uncomfortable.

As I continued to inch toward the door of the old house, my nerves started to waver. *What if Erik refuses to talk to me? What if his father answers the door? And what would I say?* I wasn't prepared for rejection, from either one of them.

A light wind scurried over my boots and around my knees while I stood and stared at the rusty doorknob. I wanted to see Erik. I wanted to see him so badly that I had thrown out all common sense and good judgment to stand on a porch in the middle of a cemetery during a massive thunderstorm. And for a moment, I was paralyzed by that thought. I wasn't scared of the dark night, the raging storm, or the ominous graveyard; I was scared about my sudden feelings for Erik. I had made such a mess of things, and I had no idea how to get things back to the way they were, or if I even wanted things to go back to how they were.

The sound of wood bending under a heavy foot cut through the wood of the door in front of me. Then the light that poured from the right window of the house wiggled, before abruptly dimming. Someone was watching me from inside. I tapped lightly on the door, two soft taps that were just loud enough to hear over the storm. No answer. I tapped two more times, slightly louder. No answer. I heard the wood bend on the other side of the door again.

"Erik? Is that you?" No answer. "Mr. Galway? I know it's late, but I saw a light on…If I could just talk to Erik for a minute…" Only the roar of angry clouds responded.

I was becoming impatient. I knew that I had no right to knock on someone's door at Lord knows what time in the morning, but then again, Erik had no right to ignore me the last few days. He had no right to talk to Lydia about me. I treaded my rain-filled boots over to the nearest window, then pressed my face to the damp glass. A minute spider scurried to a glistening web in the corner of the window while I peered inside the house.

I could see a dark figure moving in the shadows. I could hear the boards creaking, one after the other. Why wouldn't he answer the door?

In seconds the door flew open. My eyes darted to the doorway to catch a surprise. Standing in the shadows was a tall, rounded woman with a deep scowl on her face. Lightning flickered behind me, enough to highlight her deep-colored skin. Another flash illuminated the sky. I noticed a brown scarf tied around her head, leaving only the ends of tube-like hair visible in the night. With the grimace plastered across her face and the poor lighting, her hair looked like black snakes trying to escape the confines of the hair scarf. The frown on her plump lips did not waver as I tried to change my frightened expression to a polite smile. I had a feeling she could see that I was more than surprised.

"Shoo, shoo!" Dark, spotted arms flew forward through the doorway, waving frantically in the damp air. "Dis no place for chir'en be hangin' round. Go back home." Her voice was stern and full of old Cajun inflection—her long brown arms continued to shake in the space between us, like a grandmother scolding a small child.

"W-Who are you?"

"We don't be speakin' names in dese woods. Now, go home child—nuttin' good comes from nights like dese."

"But I have to see Erik. Just tell him Clara needs to talk with him," I explained.

"Don't be speakin' your name, child. Come. Come inside, hurry."

I stepped over the threshold into a dark room. The storm sounded angrier as it beat against the tin roof. I sniffed the air while the strange women walked a few steps ahead and grabbed a squeaky lantern from a hidden surface by the window. The house had a strange scent. *What is that smell?* I took a deep breath. Kerosene and formaldehyde and something else, it was a smell that was unfamiliar, yet familiar, and it masked the others. It almost smelled like incense, but I felt like it was something else. I closed my eyes while the determined women fidgeted with the glass on a seemingly broken lantern. I knew the smell; it was the same musty scent from my dream. Smoke and spice. I heard a match scratch over a rough surface, and then light erupted from within the glass of the lantern.

The house was empty.

"Who are you? Where's Erik? Where's his dad?"

"I am Maytide Gaudet."

"Maytide Gaudet? I've heard of you—you're the faith healer of Coushatta."

"You're talkin' with de last traiteuse in six parishes. We are a dyin' breed, ya know." She spoke with great pride for her title. "Now, go home child. Nuttin' good comes from nights like dese."

"Not until I speak with Erik."

"Someting' be wrong with your eyes, girl? It's just you and me here. De boy and his father been gone for some time." She moved her hands slowly over her face and scratched her freckled forehead with her long fingernails. "It's best dey gone, too. Strange dings be happenin' round dese parts."

"How did you know the Galways?"

"I only knew de boy child. He came to me a few weeks ago—askin' about you, little nightingale."

"Why? I mean, what did he ask you?"

"I see many dings, child. And I know many dings. That is why people search for me," she said. "Come—I show you someting."

I stood stiff, thinking about what she was asking of me. I shouldn't follow a stranger into the night; that's safety 101. Of course, I shouldn't have been where I was at the moment—but I was. My curiosity always worked against me—I wanted to know too much.

I stumbled out onto the deck, wrapping my arms around one another.

"Quick!" she yelled. "The storm be rollin' in some kinda fierce."

"Why should I follow you? I-I don't know you."

"But I know you, child."

She pulled me to her side and extended her arm over my head. A dark brown material draped over my hair, shielding me from nature's fury. Lightning continued to light the night sky, quickly followed by booming thunder that shattered the sound of the rain.

We dashed and darted a good mile in the woods, until we came to a small shack of a house, which, strangely enough, had a likeness to the house in the cemetery. It was like déjà vu—same small wooden porch, same rigid tin roof, even the same yellow light emanated from its dirty glass windows.

I tentatively stepped onto the porch and noticed small pieces of fish dangling from strings attached to the rafter of the roof. Maybe coming here wasn't a good idea. I had heard the rumors about the Cajun healers, just like everyone else. Traiteurs were faith healers—they used their faith, strong prayer, and remedies passed down from generation to generation to heal, but over time, many of the faith healers in Louisiana had gone bad, turning to the ways of voodoo and white magic. Alice had warned me against those ways. She had me promise to stay away from magic practices, Ouija boards, witchcraft, and anything of the sort. I could hear her warning in the back of my head, *It's the fastest way to lose yourself. Promise that you will stay far away from those practices, Clara.* At the time, it had seemed to be an easy promise to make.

Maytide must have noticed my expression. "Don't you worry, nightingale. Dis dings are nuttin' but food for de cats. De strings keep de ants from comin' to de porch."

The screen door squeaked open and then slammed behind me. The first room, which I assumed was Maytide's living room, was crammed with everything you would expect from a traiteuse. Dozens of built-in shelves held rows of glass jars and saltshakers. They almost seemed like decoration to the house—each filled with colorful substances. Powders. Liquids. Solids. One might think she was a mad scientist.

A small area to the right of the room was packed high with boxes of all sizes. All of the boxes were marked with dates and descriptions of the contents—some were marked *p.m.*, while others were marked *a.m.*. I could only make out a few words on the labels—*Alligator Tail, Strawberry Roots, Dry Potato*

Skins, Dried Pumpkin—but it was enough to know that she collected things that were much stranger than anyone I had ever known.

She shook as she trampled through the narrow living room to the kitchen. I took a deep breath before following.

In the middle of the kitchen, hanging from the hooks of a weathered potholder, were long strands of shriveled herbs, black feathers, and purple roots. The countertops were similar, storing jars—dozens of jars. I ran my fingers over the labels: *Molasses. Pickled Pig. Honey. Red Wine. Figs. Seaweed. Grape Jam. Holy Water.* Again, everything was labeled and dated.

"Why did you bring me here, Maytide?"

Maytide stayed silent as she lifted a pitcher from the countertop and then emptied its golden contents into two short glasses.

"Drink," she said.

I responded with a polite, "Thanks, but no thanks," but she insisted again.

"Drink. De hot tea is good for de body."

The warmth of the tea slid down my throat with ease and left the faint taste of ginger. It had a calming effect. I took a second sip before deciding to continue with my questions.

"Why am I here?"

Maytide looped her two spotted hands around her glass cup before speaking. "Because you need to know de truth before dey come for you."

"Who's coming for me? Am I in trouble?"

"Oh, child, don't be askin' me all de questions. Look—look."

She pointed to an old mirror that was propped against the wall behind me. The mirror appeared weathered, just like everything in the shack, and had a long jagged crack down the center. Its frame looked like it had once been thick and heavy, but now, as it leaned against the wall, it merely seemed brittle.

"Get closer—look at yourself." She walked around the table to guide my body forward. She backed away as soon as I was face-to-face with the broken mirror, staring straight into my reflection.

"I know what I look like—why…"

"Shhhh, stop with de questions. Tell me what you see."

As I faced my tired, drenched reflection in the mirror, I couldn't help but notice how pathetic I looked. I never spent much time looking at myself in the mirror—never saw the need. No matter how much makeup I added to my face, or gel I added to my hair, nothing really changed. I always looked dull, but I never realized that I looked pathetic as well. Maybe this was my new look—the look that came with being betrayed. Hurt. Or maybe it was the loneliness that stared back at me.

I was about to turn around and head back home, thinking I should have never agreed to follow her in the first place, when something incredible happened.

One side of the cracked mirror rippled.

I looked closer at my reflection, stunned by what I thought I saw. The jagged crack that flowed down the center of the mirror appeared to serve as a division between my normal reflection and a reflection that rippled from the surface of a deep blue ocean. I froze for a second, not knowing if I could believe my eyes. When I lifted a foot to take a step backward, the rippling image mimicked the action.

"Wh-What is this? What are you doing, Maytide?"

I knew that what I was seeing was not real. It was impossible. It was a hallucination. An illusion. I was sure of it. It had to be.

"Dere you are with your questions again. All you chir'en want to do is ask de questions instead of findin' de answers." Maytide was pacing about the room, arms crossed, head bobbing. "I'm not de one doin' anyting—it is you. Now tell me, what do you see?"

"I'm not sure. What I see is impossible. I see my reflection, but the mirror is changing. One side looks like me—standing here, in this room—but the other side looks different—like the surface of water, like I'm looking into a dark blue ocean." I sounded crazy explaining the image I was seeing.

"Oh yes, yes. That is good, very good. You haven't forgotten everyting."

"What are you talking about? How are you doing this?"

I stepped forward and placed both hands on the mirror, hoping I would discover the hidden trick behind the illusion. As soon as my fingertips touched the smooth surface, the mirror reverted back to its original state. Cold glass. No more rippling reflection—just me, standing in a room, with my hands pressed against an old cracked mirror. The effect was an unsettling one.

"What is happening, Maytide? Who is coming for me? Please tell me what you know," I pleaded.

I stood completely still as her body wiggled across the room to where I stood. Her hand flashed in front of me and then circled my face before she spoke in a low voice that I had to strain to hear.

"Don't worry 'bout de reflection. De mirror only reflects fragments of your true self," she said, slowly pronouncing each word carefully. "De chir'en, little nightingale. De chir'en of de dark ones be comin' for you. Dat is what we worry 'bout."

My pulse quickened.

Something about her voice—how she said dark ones sent a chill up my spine. I stood scared stiff, like I was back in the dark library of my nightmare. My eyes stayed fixated on Maytide, watching her demeanor change. The slight upward curve in her lips had dropped into a distinctive sad frown. Her eyebrows were now pushed closer together, wrinkling the loose skin between them, while her eyes looked to a distant place.

I couldn't say anything. Couldn't ask anything. I was beginning to think that I had never woken from my nightmare. Everything about the night had been strange and chilling. Maytide appeared like a character from one of those scary thriller movies Jean liked to watch. This had to be my imagination. Besides, mirrors couldn't transform into rippling water. If I woke up, I'd be right back in my bed again. My comfortable, safe bed.

Maytide's eyes narrowed, as if she could hear what I was thinking. Her distant stare slowly began to focus back to me.

"You must leave de parish. You and your aunt must go far away from dis place before dey get you."

"But this is our home. Why should we leave?"

"Dings will get bad. Dey will come for you—de process has already begun."

Process? They will come for me? I thought back to the last night I saw Erik. These were the same words he had used.

"Who are these people? And why would anyone look for me? I'm nobody."

"De dark ones are de ones dat fell from de light—de grace of God. Cast down to de lake of fire to pay for deir rebellion."

I shuttered. "Who are their children?"

"Deir children are de ones who wear de mark—de ones who gave deir souls to de night. De fallen ones."

"I don't believe you."

"Dey have many names. Fallen angels. Demons. Your generation calls dem vampyres."

"There is no such thing. Vampyres aren't real."

"Not de vampyres you read in books or see in de picture show. Dey do not have fangs. Dey do not feed on blood. Dey feed on life's essence. Dey turn de weak to evil—to de darkness. Dey will mark dem as fallen. Evil is out dere. You may not see it, but it is as real as de wind."

"I-I need to go. I shouldn't have come here."

"Here, take dis." She shuffled over to a bookshelf and grabbed a leather-bound book that was wedged between jars marked *Holy Sand* and *Lavender*.

"Read dis—cover to cover. When you finish, read it again. Do not stop readin' de book till you understand what de book is telling you."

"Understand what?"

"Dere are people in dis world who can only believe what dey see, what dey touch. Dey never believe what dey feel. You are not one of dese people. You will find everyting you need to know in dis book."

As soon as the book slid from her hands to mine, I turned and walked straight through the door. The screen door came to a squeaking close behind me. I glanced back, to see Maytide peering through the screen.

"Remember nightingale—just 'cause you can't see it, don't mean de wind don't exist." Her voice cut through the air of morning as I made my way back home.

-7-

THE BOOK

THE STORM HAD PASSED, AND THE SOFT LIGHT OF THE morning sun peeked through the trees. As I trotted back through the cemetery to the house, I noticed the Coupe was no longer in its resting place. Two lines of mud split through the green grass of the yard and trailed between the willow trees, all the way to the dirt road. Alice had already left for work.

I slid my fingers under the first step to the porch, until my hand pulled out a ball of mud and the silver key to the front door of the house. After my rendezvous with the cypress that morning, I was not about to climb through its branches again—I would use the front door like a normal person. I already had enough scratches to hide from Alice anyway.

The clock chimed as soon as I opened the door. Six o'clock, Friday morning. I had less than an hour to clean up before Jean would be waiting at the end of the road, so I sprinted up the stairs.

I followed the road down until it met the highway. Jean was already there, parked in the only grassy spot by the road, blasting her favorite pop tunes. Her style in music was much like her personality, loud, upbeat, and hard to deal with in the morning. It was even worse in the car. It was like a tsunami of zest flooded from the dashboard and poured throughout the interior of the car. Not something I wanted to be engulfed in today.

"Good morning!" Her perky voice managed to override the music before joining in on the chorus.

"Hey." I didn't bother saying anything else; she was still absorbed in her music.

"This is the song we are dancing to in our pep rally routine! Isn't it great?" The tight curls around her face bounced as she swung her head to the beat. I didn't recognize the song. It sounded like all the others. Fast rhythm. Electronic voices. Loud drums. I was still stuck on the fact that it was Friday—pep rally day, the day of ultimate enthusiasm and bursts of cheering. It was going to be a long day.

The tires slipped briefly on the highway before she turned and rolled over the rough pavement of the school parking lot. On Fridays, Jean parked in the front parking lot of the school to unload the dozens of signs she always made to decorate the gym. Today the Red River Bulldogs played our rival team, the Riverdale Wildcats, so the car was filled with extra school spirit.

I went to my first class feeling tired and lonely. When Erik was here, I would spend all class period writing notes to him, but now that he was gone, things had reverted back to the way they were. I was alone. I sunk down into my usual seat two rows away from the window and six rows back, then shuffled through my bag to grab my chemistry book. On Fridays our class periods were shortened to allow for the pep rally at the end of the day, so instead of going to the lab to learn something new, we spent the entire class period in silence filling out chapter reviews—busywork.

It took all of my energy to stay awake and to focus on the questions in front of me, but in less than twenty minutes, I had managed to jot down reasonable answers that might land me a satisfying B, at best. My hand slipped back into my bag and grabbed the leather-bound book Maytide had given me. I heard giggling from the back of the room. It was Lydia. After the stunt she had pulled at lunch the day before, I had no desire to be anywhere near her. Her presence alone bothered me.

I channeled my attention back to the small book on my desk, hoping to avoid drawing attention from anyone in the class. I sure wasn't in the mood to talk today—especially to Lydia. I flipped open the thin book to the first wrinkled page.

> *Father, please grant me the strength to spread your light. Please give me the courage to spread truth to the darkest of lands so that every shadow may be engulfed in your light. In the name of the Father, the Son, and the Holy Spirit, amen.*

It was the prayer from my dream. I quickly flipped to the front cover of the book. In the bottom right-hand corner were the letters *CC* burned into the leather. *How is this possible?* How could I have dreamed about a book I hadn't yet seen? I opened the book again and began to read through its pages.

[10]Finally, be strong in the Lord and in his mighty power. [11]Put on the full armor of God so that you can take your stand against the Devil's schemes. [12]For our struggle is not against flesh and blood, but against the rulers, against the authorities, against the powers of this dark world, and against the spiritual forces of evil in the heavenly realms.

Ephesians 6:10-12, I had read this before. Once in my dream and once in a highlighted passage of Mom's bible. I turned to the next faded page, simply to find that half of it had been victim to some kind of old red liquid spill. I was only able to make out the first four lines of a poem.

Beneath the towering castle clock
A state of darkness will unlock
The owls of time will take their flight
When evil seeps into the night.

The next page had the same dried liquid marks, smudging all of the writing except for the first two lines.

On high tides will the ocean bring
The nightingale who's lost her wings.

The poem stopped there, and so did the rest of the book. The other pages were completely blank other than the colorful red stains.

Every class seemed to whiz by—the bell would ring as soon as I had gotten comfortable in my plastic chair, and then I would silently walk down the hall to the next class. I didn't talk to anyone, I didn't meet Jean in our usual greeting spots, I didn't sit with anyone at lunch, and I didn't stop by my locker. I simply kept my first-period books with me and walked down the crowded halls of the school, like a zombie, to each class. I was going through the motions just to get through the day—just so I could get home and try to figure things out. The only things on my mind were Erik, Maytide, and the book of poems. I couldn't wait for this day to be over.

On the ride home, the silver sky began to shower the road with a light mist. I was having trouble concentrating on Jean's daily ramblings. Normally, I was considered a good listener. I always took in her dramatic stories and gave perfectly acceptable feedback, but ever since the fight with Erik—ever since he left—my world was a muffled mess. All I could think about was the last day I saw him. His words still lingered in my mind. His touch still tingled on my skin. And now, after meeting Maytide—after reading the book—I felt completely disconnected from the world I thought I knew. I was still trying to take it all in.

Jean turned right onto the long, bumpy road that stretched to our house and then killed the engine of her MINI Cooper. I was still staring at the windshield wipers when they came to a halt in the middle of the windshield. Jean broke my daze.

"Earth to Clara."

"Yeah?"

Jean raised both eyebrows and shot me one of her notorious looks. She only gave this look when she knew she'd been ignored. "I'm not really used to talkin' to myself. It makes for a long drive."

"Sorry. I just have a lot on my mind."

"Stop apologizing." Her eyebrows dropped to a more serious shape, and then she turned in her seat to face me. "You know, you're startin' to worry me. I wish you'd tell me what you're thinkin'. You say you hate Erik, but I can tell you miss him."

"I don't want to talk about him."

"So you'd rather sit and think about him?"

"No. Jean—look, I don't understand what happened with Erik. I'm beginning to think I never will. So, let me figure this out on my own." My tone came out snappy.

I turned to open the car door, but paused when Jean's voice cut through the car.

"Clara," she said. I moved my head just enough to see her worried expression.

"I'm your friend, remember?"

"I know, and you always will be. Just give me space on this one." I pushed the door open and slid out with my backpack in hand. "Don't worry about me. I'll be fine in a few weeks." We both forced a fake smile while the small car woke from its short-lived nap. In seconds, she was rolling down the highway and I was heading home—alone, through the soft rain. This was becoming an annoying reoccurrence.

-8-

RUN

My attention focused on the coupe. Our white '65 Mustang Coupe was parked next to the house, under the shadow of the giant cypress tree that overlooked my bedroom window. The sun had already moved to its resting place behind the blue and gray clouds, leaving only a few beams of light to illuminate the Coupe and the newly glossed front yard. *Alice is home already?* Strange. Maybe she was able to get out of work early for our weekend road trip. That would be a very unexpected, but pleasant surprise for the both of us. I really wanted to pick her brain—to see if she knew anything about Erik or Maytide or the book. Anything.

From a distance, the shadows hung over the house and Coupe, hiding the peeling paint and giving both a youthful, more restored appearance. It was a good look for both. As I neared the front porch, I noticed Alice's heart-shaped keychain, the one that held keys to everything imaginable, next to the prickly welcome mat. I took my first step onto the porch. There was a loud shattering sound inside the house, followed by another shatter. My skin ran cold and my heart thudded hard and fast against my rib cage. I was momentarily paralyzed by the sound. Something was wrong.

"She's protecting her," said a low, raspy voice. "She's not going to tell him where it is."

"Forget about the woman. Let him deal with her," a woman replied. She spoke with an unusual accent, far from being Southern. Her dialect was crisp and proper, but harsh all the same. "We will find the book and bring back the girl, as instructed. No exceptions."

When I looked through the window, my heart sank further into the pit of my stomach. There were countless books and papers covering the living room floor. Erik was in the middle, frantically shoveling through one of our many built-in bookcases. He was wearing his sunglasses.

A tall red-haired woman stood to his left, adding to the pile by flinging knickknacks from the ledge of the fireplace. She matched Erik, wearing dark clothes and sunglasses.

I felt the stinging fear like I had felt in my dream. I tried to grasp the concept of what was happening. Erik was back. He was in our house. He was not alone. *Where is Alice?* I almost jumped out of my skin when I heard something heavy fall to the floor near the window. The house was being wrecked.

I glued myself to the outside wall of the house and then slowly bent down until my butt sat against the damp porch. *This can't be happening.* I reminded myself to breathe. *Is this the danger I was warned about?* I would never forgive myself if anything happened to Alice. I had to get inside. I had to find her.

I was afraid one of them would hear me, but I was able to grab Alice's keys and glide through the door undetected. Keeping my body as close to the wall as possible, I slid into the wedge between the staircase and the wall of the next room and then squatted in the shadows. I raised my head slightly to peek through the space between the wooden rails.

They were moving toward the kitchen, to make a bigger mess, I presumed. Cabinets opened, and then pots banged against the kitchen floor. This was my chance to get upstairs—to look for Alice. I had no clue what constituted a good plan—this just seemed like my only option.

I crept up the entire flight of stairs without being heard. I ran straight to Alice's room. Her room had been turned upside down. Clothes. Papers. Books. Photos. Pillows. Everything was tossed on the floor. But there was no Alice. I ran to her bathroom—no Alice. I tugged open her closet door—no Alice. Maybe she was in my room. I quietly tiptoed my way out of her bedroom, but paused just before I made it to my room.

He saw me. He met my frightened eyes, looking pleased to see that I was standing at the top of the stairs, frozen like a deer in headlights. I had to tell my body to move. *Just move. Move. Move, now!* The words came out in the form of a meager grunt as I sprinted toward the door to my bedroom.

"She's here!" I heard him scream as he trampled up the steps.

He got up the stairs faster than I anticipated. I slammed the door and turned the lock just in time. My belongings had been tossed around like a tornado had touched down—all my posters were ripped from the wall. I waded through my things until I reached the window. Still, no Alice.

I flung open the window and heaved myself to the veranda. I'm not sure how I managed to get to the ground so fast, not sure if I jumped or fell, but either way I landed on the metal roof of the Coupe.

I rolled to the side of the car and yanked at the door handle. Thankfully the car was left unlocked—the key pushed right into the ignition. I turned the engine over again and again. It groaned, but it wouldn't crank. I smelled gas. I had flooded the engine.

A loud thud came from the metal roof of the Coupe. Erik had followed me down—he was on the car. He was grinning when he looked down through the windshield. We were only separated by glass. Just glass. He knew that, and I knew that. I frantically slapped the door locks down. I stomped the pedal to the floor and twisted the key again—the car finally rumbled to life. My foot slid from the clutch, causing the car to jump forward. The wheels spun mud and gravel everywhere, but it didn't matter. I was moving.

I kept my foot flat against the pedal and jerked right on the steering wheel—the car soared around the old cypress, fishtailing inches away from the large tree trunk. I was taken back by the excitement—with the adrenaline pumping through my veins, I almost felt light-headed. I knew he was still on the car; I heard him pound against the metal. The woman started to chase after us, her hair bouncing as she ran from the porch. She was fast, really fast.

The gears of the transmission grunted and grinded as I accelerated down our dirt road. I steered into every pothole, hoping to see him fly from the car. His arm slipped to the windshield, and I could tell that he was scuffling for a better hold. But he still held on. I had one more shot to lose him. If I could turn hard enough onto the freeway, I might just sling him off.

I could see the highway coming up in the distance. I fastened my seat belt and held the steering wheel for dear life. I fumbled with the clutch and shifted once more before shooting the RPM into the red. I used both hands to cut hard onto the highway.

His body flew over the windshield, splintering the glass down the middle and bouncing off the side of the car. I had won.

My hands wouldn't stop shaking while I sped along the misty highway. This wasn't happening. This couldn't be happening. *Why are they after me? Was Alice kidnapped?* My mind couldn't wrap around either idea. We didn't own anything of real value, and Alice didn't have an enemy in the world. *What did they do with her? What do they want? And why are they after me? Think. Think.*

I needed help. I didn't have a cell phone, and the nearest phone was across the river. I didn't see them behind me anymore—I could make it.

The mist thickened to a hard rain. Of course. I felt blindly for the lever to turn on the wipers, then flipped on the headlights. *I just need to concentrate on driving. Focus.* The speedometer was steadily increasing. Fifty mph. Fifty-five mph. Sixty mph. I would have help in no time, I thought. But I was wrong.

My eyes slowly fluttered opened, but all I could see was an upside-down world. There was a loud ringing in my ears and pressure building in my head. I looked up. My hair dangled from my head and rested on the ceiling that was battered and beaten into the muddy earth. I looked to the shattered driver's side window. Rain pounded in and formed puddles on the metal ceiling. I glanced up at my white-knuckled hands. My hands were bleeding now, but were still clinging to the grooves in the leather steering wheel. I loosened my grip and slid my shaky hands along my sides. No broken bones, but a nice whelp had already formed on my ribs where the floor shift had detached and pushed against my side. I was still strapped against the leather seat. I reached to my right side and forced my thumb into the release button—nothing happened. I yanked the seat belt while I jabbed at the release—nothing. The belt was jammed.

Only seconds ago, I had slammed on the brakes too fast and jerked the steering wheel too hard. I had flipped the Coupe off the road and rolled clear down the ditch. *But why?* Erik had been in the middle of the road with the girl, perched on a black and silver motorcycle, blocking my way out. They were just sitting there in the rain—head turned sideways with their black shades in place. *How did they catch up to me?* It didn't matter now. I needed to get loose. I needed to get out of the car. I needed to run.

I pulled at the seat belt, throwing the weight of my body into it, until something snapped. I didn't take time to see what had broken I just grabbed my bag and crawled my way out of the metal heap. My side was hurting now.

I took a step away from the car to look through the rain. I didn't see them. I didn't see anyone. I took another step away from the car and used my hands to shield my eyes from the rain. That's when I saw them.

They were standing next to the motorcycle, studying the land. Fortunately for me, the ditches of Louisiana were too soft for any machine to drive through—that's what caused the Coupe to slide so far away from the highway. They would have to catch me on foot.

I placed a hand on my side and began to stagger away. I looked over my shoulder to see them sliding down into the ditches.

I started to run. If I could just make it to the swamp, I would have a chance. I weaved through the high grass and inches of mud until I reached the edge of the woods. I clung to the first tree trunk in the path and squeezed it tight while I caught my breath. They were getting closer, but I was almost there.

A beam of moon cut through the branches of the trees and shone on the path before me. Faded green moss hung from the tree branches and swayed like dark tinsel on an eerie Christmas tree. The spongy land began to sink below my feet to form pools of algae-filled water. Each time I lifted my foot from the soft soil, suction from the mud would pull at my shoes. It didn't take many steps before the mud had sucked them completely from my feet, but I kept moving.

Branches snapped in the blackness of the forest, followed by the sound of splashing water—they were near. I looked at the algae-blanketed water before me and then plunged forward into the floating greenery. The warm water quickly rose from my ankles to my chest as I waded through the marshy land. Through the trees I caught a small shimmer of light; a small shimmer of hope awaited me. Just a little bit further. I gritted my teeth as my bare feet slid across slippery surfaces at the bottom of the swamp. No telling what creatures or trash my feet were coming in contact with.

Whispers came from behind. I quietly veered off into a pile of floating shrubbery and sunk down into the water until my head poked just above the surface like a turtle. They were getting closer.

"Is she still out here?" the redhead questioned.

"Oh yes, she's still here—I can smell her fear," Erik said. "Check the borders of the swamp. She couldn't have gone far." His voice made my skin crawl.

Something in the shrubs moved, and I reacted with a sudden jerk in the water.

"Did you hear that?" The woman spoke again. "Give me your flashlight."

I quietly waded out from the shrubbery as a beam of light skimmed the water's surface. As the light neared, I took a deep breath and lowered my face underwater. I kept my eyes tightly shut to keep out the muggy water, but through my lids I saw the light pass over the surface. I held my breath as long as I could before resurfacing. A mutter and a crackle came from the muddy shore—they had moved down the edge of the swamp. There was no way I could get ahead of them on land now, but if I stayed in the water—I just might make it.

I waded out into the middle of the water, completely away from the shrub-lined edges. At this time of night, the snakes and alligators rested near the banks and the fallen cypress trees. As long as I kept my distance, they shouldn't bother me. I just needed to push my way through the muck, to the shack. Fergus had already moved into the Swamp Tours shack—he would be there, and he would help me. I began to swim.

I heaved my weight out of the water and rolled my aching body onto the wooden deck. I laid flat on the rough surface while I steadied my breathing. It was a relief to be out of the dark water. I looked back to the bank—I could see the faint light from the flashlight still skimming the earth. I had maybe ten minutes before they would be here; I had a feeling they would thoroughly investigate the shack.

I crawled over to the old door of the shack and peeped in through the fogged window. Fergus was sitting by a small fire, reading, like always. I tapped on the glass.

"Fergus!" I lowered my voice a bit more, "Let me in—hurry."

I saw a small twinkle in his eye as he hobbled from his quiet place by the fire to the door. As soon as the door cracked open, I slid in and grabbed his shoulders.

"I am so sorry I've put you in danger. I-I need your help, Fergus. I don't know what to do."

"You're soaking wet, child. Are you all right?"

"No, I'm not." I was still breathing heavy from the swim. "Alice is missing, and Erik and this woman, they were in the house. They took her, Fergus. I don't know where, but they took her. And now they are after me—and I flipped the car, and they followed me. I don't know what they want. I just kept running. I waded over here—but they are on their way. We have to go." I paused, still frazzled from everything that had happened. "I know this must sound crazy, but you have to believe me—it's not safe here." Nothing I said made sense, even to me.

"I believe you. Just take a deep breath. Let me get a knife."

"A knife? Did you not hear me?" I bent over slightly to calm my breathing. "We need to get out of here."

"Everything will be okay. Let's first take care of these leeches."

"Leeches?" I immediately looked down to my feet. A slimy brown tube was wedged in the crease by my big toe. I glanced to my other foot—two more leeches were stuck to the top of my foot. I flinched and let out a gasp.

"Get them off. Get them off," I begged while I slapped my hands at the top of my feet.

"Now calm down—if you slap them off, the leeches will regurgitate into the wound. We don't want you to get an infection." Fergus quickly shuffled over to the small kitchen part of the shack, grabbed a knife, and motioned for me to follow him to the table. "Sit, sit. We will take the airboat to town. Just let me get these suckers off your feet."

I sat in the chair, eyeing the window, while he slid the knife under the anterior sucker of each leech. I cringed in disgust as he popped the squirmy worms from my skin. After the leeches were off and stomped dead, Fergus limped over to the cabinet in the corner of the room. He opened the lower cabinet drawers and grabbed a brown sack. In my peripheral vision, I saw his aged hand toss a set of rattling keys into the bag, along with something wrapped in a woolen cloth.

"What's that?" I questioned.

"Something you will need—I will only be a minute. Grab the keys from the table and head for the boat. I'll be right behind you."

"All right, please hurry. They weren't far behind me."

I swiped the keys from the table's wooden surface and flew through the door. My shoulders tensed as the old boards of the deck moaned and creaked with every step. The deck had spent centuries exposed to the harsh elements of Louisiana's swamp waters, not to mention the countless times the deck had been used as breaks for the airboat—but it chose tonight to complain about it.

I looked over my shoulder to the woods. The light was closer. The minute Fergus had promised had already stretched to several. What was taking him so long? What was he packing? I struggled to stay calm.

Before I jumped into the boat, I tiptoed around to the fillet station that was connected to the side of the shack and swiped an old cutting knife. I leaned over the cutting board and peeked through the small, dusty window that still beamed light from the fire. I could see Fergus still limping around, collecting items in his brown bag. I lightly tapped the knife on the glass and gave him a nervous look. He nodded and then finally closed his bag.

I took long, quiet strides over to the edge of the deck and stepped onto the aluminum surface of the boat. I collapsed into the damp driver's seat and tried to recover a sense of tranquility. The keys and the knife rattled together in my lap, while my right leg shook with anxiety. I kept my eyes glued to the deck, waiting for Fergus to round the side of the shack at any moment.

I glanced back to the wooded area—I couldn't see the light anymore. A disturbing thought entered my head—it had been over ten minutes since I'd rolled onto the wooden deck. They could already be here lurking around the shack. Through the loud singing of the crickets and frogs, I heard the familiar moaning of the deck floor.

"Oh, Clara, Clara, Clara. Why are you making this difficult?"

My body tensed. They were here. I tried to contain my nerves as I watched two slender figures round the corner of the shack.

"Did you think you could outrun us? Or were you just wanting to play?" Erik questioned again. His shades were still on, but I could feel his eyes on me.

I carefully let the knife fall between my legs so that it was completely hidden. It was the closest thing I had to a weapon. It would have to do.

"What did you do with Alice?" I tried to sound strong, but the anxiety was clear in my voice. I was afraid of what their answer might be, but I had to know. I couldn't lose my aunt; she was all I had—the only family I knew.

"We just had a little talk with her." The redhead spoke with such a sweet tone, it almost sounded innocent.

"Tell me where she is!" I yelled.

"I don't believe you are in a position to make demands," he said.

"What do you want?" My lips trembled as I glared at the evil version of the Erik I thought I once knew.

"I told you I would come for you, did I not?"

"Why? I'm nobody. If you are doing this for money, you should know we don't have any money."

The redhead and Erik chuckled before he continued. "It's not about money. We just need you."

He stepped over the side of the boat and placed one hand on my shoulder and braced himself with the other on the back of the seat. I felt light-headed as soon as his fingers touched my skin.

"This doesn't have to hurt—if you just cooperate," he said.

Out of the corner of my eye I saw a shadow creeping toward the girl. Fergus. He was slowly making his way onto the deck with his cane in one hand

and his bag in the other. I lowered my arms to my lap and discreetly slid the hidden knife under my hand.

Whack!

In a split second, Fergus had knocked the redhead to her knees. I promptly turned the swivel chair and kicked with all my strength. My heel caught Erik straight in the chest. The air boat rocked from the movement, causing him to fall against its aluminum floor. He scrambled to grab the side to push himself from the floor. I stood from the chair and raised my leg for another kick. He caught my foot, pulling me down by his side. I struggled to get up from the floor. But he was too strong.

He pinned me against the side of the boat, pressing my sore side. I lashed at him with the knife, but it quickly flew from my hand to the deck. He pushed me harder against the boat, so that the aluminum cut into my back. His fingers latched around my throat in an unbreakable hold. My eyes darted to Fergus for help. But it was no use. The women had risen from the deck, and she stood between us—furious. And she had the knife now. My eyes began to water as I struggled for air. I was scared for Fergus. I was scared for myself.

Erik lifted me from the boat by my neck and flung me to the hard surface of the deck. He looked down, pleased by the pain he had caused.

This couldn't be it for me, I thought. I was exhausted and still gasping for oxygen, but I was not ready to give up. I was not ready to die. Not by his hands, by his terms—not without a fight.

Fergus had knocked the knife from the woman's hand; it was only a few feet from me now. If I stretched, I could reach it. I had to go for it.

I swung my leg as hard and as high as I could, jabbing it right between his legs. He dropped to the deck with a moan. I grabbed the fillet knife and forced the blade through the flesh of his hand. The knife drove down hard into the wood below it.

"You whore!" he yelled furiously as he grabbed at his hand.

A loud crack came from behind. I turned just in time to see the fiery redhead fly into the water, landing with a big splash. We were winning.

Fergus threw his cane and bag into the boat and then helped me over the side. We could hear Erik screaming from the deck as he pulled at the knife that joined his hand to the wood.

The propeller of the boat buzzed as soon as Fergus turned the key. The air from the blades drowned out the sound of the screams as we propelled away from the shack.

"Are you hurt?"

"I'll be all right," I replied while pulling my flying hair back. "I'm so sorry I brought you into all of this. Are you okay?"

"Yes, dear, I'm fine. But you needn't apologize. We need to get you to the library. Things are much worse than I imagined." He still spoke with the gentle voice that I knew and loved, but it was different somehow, more protective.

"What about Alice? We need to help her. We need to go to the police."

"This is not a matter for the police, dear. I know where Alice will be—and it's no place they can go."

"How do you know this? Where is she?"

"You still don't remember anything, do you?" he asked as though he already knew it to be true. I could see a hint of sadness behind his squinted eyes.

"You are starting to scare me, Fergus. Please, tell me what I need to know."

"Let's get you to the library first."

-9-

REALITY

YELLOW LIGHT FROM THE STREETLAMPS LIT THE ENTRANCE to the library, casting shadows of waving trees on its peeling beige exterior. This old place was my second home.

We entered into a very still library. There were no sounds of whispers, papers turning, or books closing—only the sound of Fergus's shoes against the marble floor. As soon as the door shut behind us, Fergus locked the dead bolts and then wrapped a chain around the door handles. We weren't going anywhere for the night.

I followed him through the second pair of doors that led into the hall of books, but stopped when he turned down the poetry aisle. I hadn't been in the library since my last nightmare, and to be honest, I was still shaken by it.

Fergus turned around to gauge the distance between his bottom and the small chair of the wooden desk. It was the same aisle and the same desk from my dream. He slowly sunk into the seat and leaned back. The chair tilted, clicking until it finally locked at a slanted angle to the floor.

That's when I noticed the bookcase in front of the desk crack open.

"Fergus," I said automatically, "what is this?"

He carefully stood from the desk and pushed the bookcase open. "It's a secret chamber, dear. Constructed for times such as these." He motioned with a nod of his head to trust him.

"Go on," he insisted. "Take a look."

I walked past Fergus, into the chamber, with the curiosity of a child.

The room was larger than I had expected, bigger than my own bedroom, but seemed small due to the lack of windows. A foldout bed hid in the back corner of the room, next to a dozen cases of bottled water and a broken wicker chair.

Fergus directed me to the left, where a rugged bench was pressed against the pale wall, and then scooted the bench a few inches away from the wall so that it sat catty-corner to the opening we had entered.

"Have a seat, darling," he said.

He waited until I was completely settled next to him before saying another word. "I know that everything that has happened to you in the past few weeks has been difficult for you to understand. I can see the uncertainty in your eyes, and I can see that you doubt what you used to believe." Fergus looked sideways with a look of sincerity. "Clara, there are things in this world that are very hard to explain, but it is crucial for you understand."

"Just tell me what's going on. Why is this happening to me? And how do you know so much?"

Fergus cut my questions short. "Do you remember the story of the darkness?"

"Yes, of course, the story of good and evil—of light and darkness. You tell that one practically every other week."

"I'm pleased you were listening." Fergus paused for a moment, just long enough to run the back of his aged hand over his forehead. "The stories were not entirely stories, dear."

I sat still, taking in every word.

"Those stories tell a history. A history of a place that is as real as this night. It is here where you must know what you believe—you must fight against the darkness," he said. Before I could form any kind of question, Fergus leaned in toward me and placed both of his warm hands on each side of my face. "These stories are your history, child."

My lips were open in disbelief. As I gazed up into his tender eyes, he said very softly, "You must believe. You are no stranger to these lands."

I shook my head free of his hands and quickly stood up.

"Why are you trying to fill my head with these ideas? I don't need your stories right now. Alice is missing! And someone is chasing us, for Pete's sake!"

Fergus was now sitting very stiff, like he was in deep thought. I could see the sadness in his eyes again. "This must be hard for you to take in, but you must try to remember," he said.

I focused on the black marble floor, trying hard to hold back my emotions. I could feel my eyes burning and the pressure building behind them. I watched as the white specks on the marble blurred into long, flowing streaks. I took a slow breath and signaled with my hand that I was ready to talk.

"Fergus, what you're telling me is impossible and cruel." I held my hands together so that I could concentrate on exactly what I wanted to say. "A part of me would love for your stories to be real," I sighed. "I want to live in a world where I know who I am—a place where I know my past. But I don't. I live here, in reality. This is real."

Fergus slowly raised himself from the bench and took two steps toward me. "Day after day I wanted to tell you—there is more to your life than this." He reached into his pocket and pulled out a folded woolen piece of fabric.

"This belongs to you," he said.

I reluctantly took the neatly folded piece of fabric from his hands. The wool was brown with age and wrapped around something small and hard.

"Do not look inside this cloth until you are ready for the truth. When that time comes, I will have one last story to tell you," he said delicately with a soft smile.

Fergus leaned in one last time and planted a small kiss on my forehead. "For now, you should rest. Tomorrow will be a big day," he said. "Tomorrow we leave this place." Then he shuffled away.

I sat there watching the distance grow further between us, until he closed the wall behind him. I was alone again. Alice was gone. Erik was evil. And Fergus was filling my head with fairy tales. I didn't know what or who to believe anymore.

I fell asleep that night wondering if I would ever see Alice again. If the one life I knew would ever be the same. I reminded myself that I couldn't lose hope. I had to believe that everything would be okay—that tomorrow just might bring a better day.

-10-

SCARLET HEIGHTS

WE TOOK A CAB TO BOSSIER CITY EARLY THAT MORNING. Bossier City was bigger than Coushatta—had better shopping, more restaurants, and an airport. I had been here a few times with Alice and Fergus, but unlike those times, we weren't here to eat or to shop.

We flew out of Bossier City at 11:00 a.m. that Saturday morning. I had never flown before, so it was quite the experience. The plane was larger than I imagined, but inside felt like a small, overcrowded bus. The seats were high and stiff, the floor space was minimal, but the view was fascinating to me. Once the initial fear of being thirty-five thousand feet in the air wore off, I almost enjoyed it.

The plane landed in Houston, Texas, where we ran through the airport to catch our connecting flight to Chicago, Illinois. We would have one more plane switch in Newark, New Jersey, before we were on the plane that would take us to Ireland.

Running from terminal to terminal was hectic and tiring. Pure adrenaline kept me awake through the first two plane rides, but that adrenaline was wearing off. Before the New Jersey plane had even left the runway, my eyes had closed, and I was drifting into a dream.

There was a girl—a small girl—running barefoot into the night. As she darted around the rocks, her long cinnamon tinted hair flew up and around a bright red cloak. I called to her desperately—*"Stop! Wait!"*—but she kept running toward the edge of the cliff. I tried to move toward her, but my feet were too heavy to move. The harder I tried to run, the less ground I covered.

"Please...wait," I pleaded again. *"Where are you going?"* I noticed a short giggle floating through the wind as it pushed by me.

She did not stop. I tried to plead with her again, but this time my voice was gone. Not a sound or word escaped my lips. My arms reached for her, but she could not see.

The young girl had finally made her way to the edge and was staring down into the raging sea. I could feel panic rushing through my body as I realized I could not save her. Suddenly, the wind stopped blowing, and all was quiet. As her hair lay to rest against her cloak, she slowly turned around.

"I must go home," she said with a small grin.

All I could do was motion for her to stop, but she simply extended her arms into the night air and smiled. Then, with her back to the sea, she let herself fall over the cliff. She fell in slow motion. I held my breath and watched helplessly as her small body fell over the edge into darkness. Everything immediately turned pitch-black.

I woke up with my sweaty forehead plastered to the plastic window of the airplane. Once my eyes focused, I could see rich green mountains and a rocky coastline through a light film of fluffy clouds. *Ireland.*

The colors of the countryside were bright, even from high above the clouds. It was a beautiful sight, almost beautiful enough to take my mind off the nightmare. There was no mistake; the dreams were getting worse.

"What do you think?" Fergus asked, pointing out the window.

"It's nothing like I've ever seen."

It really was enchanting. Something about the blue of the water and the green of the land made it appear like a flawless dream. It would have made a perfect postcard.

"What time is it?" I asked through a much-needed yawn.

"Nine a.m.," he replied. "Sunday morning."

The plane landed in Belfast, Ireland, safely and on time. Since we didn't have luggage to claim, we made it through the airport fairly quickly. We didn't stop until we walked through the sliding doors at the entrance.

Fergus dropped his brown carry-on bag to his side and skimmed his eyes over the people walking the sidewalks. He was looking for someone.

I stood there quietly gazing at the sky and listening to the sounds of Ireland. I could hear birds chirping over the loud putter of taxi-car engines. The sky was a smooth baby-blue color with pink and orange clouds drifting across its horizon.

I eavesdropped as people walked past. The accent here was very different than I had expected. Words were pronounced with hard consonants and with a strange rhythm. It was hard to understand what everyone was saying at first, but the harder I listened, the easier it got.

After standing there for a good ten minutes, a fancy black limousine pulled up to the curb. It was an older car—a classic. The body of the car was long and curved, like a wave pushing forward. It had protruding round lights on the front, a large grill, and a silver hood ornament of a woman leaning into the wind like an angel.

The driver of the car, a man in a black suit, stepped out and walked directly to us. He was middle-aged, fairly tall, with square shoulders. He had a nice smile.

"Calahan?" he asked in a rich Irish accent.

"Yes, yes," Fergus responded.

"Good morning, sir—miss." He tipped his head slightly and grinned. "I am here to drive you to Scarlet Heights."

"Scarlet Heights," I whispered under my breath. "What kind of a place is Scarlet Heights?"

"It is a manor, dear." Fergus responded. His cheeks rounded with a grin. "And someone very special lives there. Someone I've been waiting for you to meet."

The driver stepped between us to grab the brown bag Fergus had set beside him, and then loaded it in the small trunk of the car. He quickly darted to the back door, swung it open, and stood tall with a pleasant smile.

"Nice day for seeing the sights," he said cheerfully.

"Nice day, indeed," Fergus replied.

As soon as we slid into the car, the driver shut the door in place and then quickly trotted over to the driver's side. He seemed enthusiastic about the upcoming journey.

Our driver, who insisted we call him Duffy, veered and honked his way out of the airport traffic, then turned to take a narrow, less-traveled road. I clutched my seat belt a few times as the car whizzed by oncoming traffic. It was going to take some time getting use to driving on the left side of the road.

I forgot all about it when the view from the side window changed from plain green countryside to a rocky land that dropped into the ocean. I rolled down my window to smell the rich, salty air for the first time.

The car slowly inclined, giving us a far better view of the ocean. I placed my arm on the window seal to hold my head as I studied the new scenery.

The ocean stretched out across the horizon and kissed the painted sky. Waves traveled all the way from the edge of the earth just to explode at the rocky shore. Seagulls welcomed them by swooping down from the sky to meet their white, foamy spray.

My head was still balanced against the open window seal when I saw Scarlet Heights for the first time.

Scarlet Heights was by all means a castle. It towered in the colorful sky, shading the land around it. Hundreds of red rosebushes were in bloom along the stone wall that led to its gates. Green vines climbed the outer walls, while more red roses colored the courtyard.

My mouth automatically dropped open in awe at its greatness.

"And that's why they call it Scarlet Heights," Fergus said.

As the car came to a stop in the circular courtyard, I noticed a woman standing at the door, dressed in a flowing golden dress, admiring the ruby color of the roses. Her eyes sparkled when her attention turned to us. In seconds Fergus had his arms wrapped around her, completely covering her body with his.

It wasn't until they parted that I realized how stunning the woman was. Her green eyes were kind and her smile warm. There was a slight tint of peach lipstick remaining on her lips, which went well with the soft gold color of her skin and hair. She had to be nearly Fergus's age, but you wouldn't have guessed it at first or second glance.

"Clara," she said as her hand lightly touched my shoulder. She looped an arm around my head and pulled me close to her. "I can't believe you are finally here."

"You've got a beautiful place," I said as I subconsciously pulled away. "Have we met before?"

She shot a concerned look at Fergus and then back to me.

"Of course, dear. I'm your—"

"Norma," Fergus interrupted. "Her name is Norma. You knew her when you were young."

"How did I know you exactly?"

There was an awkward silence for a moment. "Let's go inside, dear. We should get you settled in before we catch up."

The inside of the manor was just as striking as the outer walls. The floor was tiled with different shades of yellow stone that complemented the walls. Golden drapes shaded the windows, and red decorative rugs covered the floor.

Norma walked beside me with her long yellow dress gliding over the patterns on the floor. I was dressed in a printed white T-shirt, black shorts, and black sneakers, an outfit I had quickly bought between connecting flights. I automatically felt underdressed.

"We are throwing a party tonight, in your honor. I understand you won't remember their faces, but everyone is dying to see you!" She paused for a moment, allowing me to walk slightly ahead of her.

"Everyone?"

"You used to play in these halls as a young girl. You especially loved sliding down the staircase. Do you remember that? You were so little then. You would count each step on the way up and then slide down. I was scared to death the first time I saw you fly down them. You would just laugh and laugh! Now look at you. You are a beautiful woman!"

I was interested in knowing how my family was connecting to all of this—to this place specifically, but I didn't feel like prying would be appropriate. Not until I unpacked, at least.

"So I guess our families were close, huh?"

Norma smiled as we took our first step on the staircase. "Closer than you know, child."

We climbed the dark staircase, following the red carpet that lined the steps. After passing several large windows that looked over a green courtyard, we then turned and went up another flight of stairs. These steps ended on the second floor. Altogether I counted thirty-five steps.

"Your room is right down this hall. The one with the double doors," she said, pointing to the right.

I opened the doors to find a room fit for a queen.

The walls were pale yellow, with crown molding. Folds of scarlet drapes shut in the window to the right; to the front were clear panes of glass opening up to an ocean view. A window seat, neatly cushioned to match the drapes, sat against the floor-length panes. A long golden material fell from the ceiling, creating a canopy over a frilly bed, while two fancy lamps stood tall on both sides.

"This is my room?" I questioned in disbelief at my good fortune.

"Of course. This was your favorite room."

"I've slept here before?"

"Many times."

"Oh."

"We can find you another room if you feel uncomfortable...I just thought—"

"The room is great, Norma. I really mean it," I said, quickly interrupting her thought.

"There's a powder room through that door." She pointed to a door hidden in the molding on the left side of the room, while walking over to the bed. "The wardrobe inside contains a few clean clothes. I can take you shopping tomorrow for some new ones if you like."

She caught my eyes darting to the bed as she spoke.

"Oh, Clara, I'm sorry. Here you are, tired, and I'm carrying on about clothes. You've had a long trip—I can only imagine how exhausted you must be. Why don't you lay down and take a little nap before our guests arrive, hmm?"

Tired was an understatement. I simply nodded and smiled politely.

"If you're sure you don't mind," I said, "it would be nice to take a bath and lay down for a few hours."

"You take as long as you like, sweetie," she insisted while she made her way back through the door. "I'm going to drive into town to pick up a few things for tonight. I'll check on you when I return."

"Thanks."

"I'll see you in a bit..."

After a nice warm bath, I toweled off and slipped into one of the nightgowns from the wardrobe. I went straight to the bed and drifted to sleep in seconds.

Six hours later, my eyes opened after dreaming that Alice was taken. Then I remembered she was taken—that the nightmare was real. Alice was still missing, and Fergus had brought me here to find her. *And where was I?* Northern Ireland. I was staying in Northern Ireland, in a manor—no, in a castle—called Scarlet Heights.

I hopped from my bed to sit on the red cushion under the deep-set windowsill. Norma was right about the view, I loved it. Scarlet Heights towered over a steep cliff that dropped into rocky water. Green grass carpeted the ground, surrounding the castle and fading into rock as it neared this steep drop-off. From my window you could see miles and miles of the deep blue sea held in place by a rocky coastline. The dangerous waters looked tranquil through the glass pane. I almost felt at ease watching the waves crash against the shore.

About the time my mind drifted, Norma walked into the room.

"How was your nap?" she asked in her sweet voice.

I cleared my throat a bit before answering politely, "It was exactly what I needed."

"Good. You look very rested."

"Yes, ma'am."

"I hope you don't mind that I picked up a few things for you while I was in town. I thought you might like to dress up tonight since everyone is coming to see you. Fergus said the two of you left in quite a hurry—didn't have time to pack, he said." As she finished the sentence, she opened a large box and pulled out a simple, yet elegant red dress. "I hear red never goes out of style."

"It's perfect." I bounced from the window seat and ran to her.

"And we can't forget the shoes." She tilted the box very slightly. Sitting at the bottom on crisp white tissue paper were a pair of red velvet high heels.

"Oh, thank you—but, this is way too much." I laid the dress on the end of the bed, while she placed the box and shoes to its side. She quietly walked over to me.

"I've waited for this day for many years. It brings me great joy to have you here." She paused long enough to sweep her hand over my cheek. "Nothing will ever be too much for our Clarabella." She reached around my head and pulled me in for a hug. I quickly wrapped my arms around her.

While my head rested on her shoulder, I inhaled her sweet smell of lavender and sunshine. I could see another smile form on her kind face.

I looked right into her glistening eyes. "Thank you," I said. "Thank you for everything."

-11-

SCARLET REFLECTIONS

EVERYWHERE I TURNED THERE WAS ANOTHER FACE GREETING me with a smile. I had said *hello* and *nice to meet you* hundreds of times and had been the official receiver of hugs and handshakes throughout the night. Once everyone seemed to calm down and talk among one another, I was able to slip away from the crowd. I weaved my way through the many groups that had gathered, until I saw the back of the hall. I was drawn to the round silver doors and two floor-length windows.

Fergus stood next to one of the rose-colored panes, staring out into the night. He moved every few seconds to take small sips from his glass of punch.

"Need company?" I asked as I walked to him.

"You look beautiful tonight, Clara," Fergus said. His fingers tapped against the glass in his hand as he turned to reveal an award-winning smile. In some way I felt like he was proud of me.

"You should be enjoying the party, not hanging around an old man like me," he said.

"Stop saying you're old, 'cause you're not." I shook my head while clearing my throat. We both looked out into the crowd of guests. All of them seemed to be so happy.

"All these people, they know me, but I don't remember a single face. I feel so out of place." I noticed his smile fade, so I hurriedly brushed my hair from my shoulder and gave an enthusiastic grin. "But the food is great," I added.

He chuckled. "That's the Clara I know."

We stood side by side, looking through the window at the night sky. Fergus continued to sip on his punch until it was almost gone.

"Fergus," I said, breaking the trance, "you said you knew where they took Alice. Why won't you tell me?"

He tilted his head down and looked up through droopy eyes. "Sometimes it's too hard to hear the truth, dangerous even. I need you to trust me, Clara. Trust that I will do everything in my power to keep you safe and to bring her back."

"I do trust you. It's just...nothing makes sense. I feel lost."

As I turned my head to avoid his heartfelt gaze, my attention fell on a painting on the other side of the room. It was alone, centered in the middle of the wall. It's wide golden frame made it stand out even more against the shadowed wall. I wasn't sure how I had missed it before.

"Is that you?" I walked toward the painting, putting our conversation on hold. "And Norma?"

Before he could answer, I was close enough to see the truth for myself. The painting was a portrait of Norma and Fergus, with Scarlet Heights in all of its glory. They both held a loving gaze, with their arms holding each other. *How did I miss this? Fergus and Norma?* I thought he was a widower.

"Yes," he said from across the room.

"Why did you…?" My brain was trying to trace back to all of the times he had spoken about missing his wife. He never once mentioned that she was still alive.

"It was the only way."

"Stop saying that. Only way for what?"

He looked down at the bottom of his empty glass, not saying a word.

"For what, Fergus?"

"To protect my granddaughter," he said, and then clarified. "It was the only way to keep you safe."

Fergus is my grandfather. I directed my gaze toward the window nearest the painting. There was only silence while we each waited for the other to speak. A part of me wanted to throw my arms around him and never let go, but the other part, the more prominent part, was angry. I was hurt by the lies, by the secrets.

"Don't be upset," he said, reaching for my hand.

"All this time…" I swallowed, clearing the lumps from my throat while I backed away. "I can't do this right now."

I felt his eyes on my back, following me until I made my way into the dark hallway. The stairs seemed endless as I stomped to my bedroom. I*s anything in my life real? Or is it all a lie?* I could actually feel my face getting hot again from frustration. I swung the heavy door to my room open, and a nice rush of air cooled the heat on my skin.

I'd been naive all along. *Is Alice even my aunt? Is she really missing?* I shuffled my feet over to the windowsill to sulk against the cold glass. A loose curl fell to my face as I watched the dark waves of the ocean ripple effortlessly across the deep abyss. It made sense now, why he brought me here. They were my father's parents. This is where we lived.

I watched the waves for hours, trying to find logic behind the secrets, when my eyes spotted someone in the darkness. Someone from the party, I imagined.

I stood up to get a better look. That's when I saw her face. This someone wasn't just a guest from the party. It was a young girl. And she was walking straight for the edge of the cliff. Just like my dream.

How can this be happening? Am I dreaming again? She had the same long brown hair. The same oversized scarlet cape. She stopped when she reached the edge, turned, and looked up at the window. Then she was gone.

I panicked. I grabbed my bag and flew down the stairs. The hall that had been crowded once before had cleared to only a few small groups of loud guests. I managed to slip past the vigorous chatter to the empty hall with the wide silver doors.

The crisp night air glided around me as I stood outside the walls. I threw my bag over my shoulders and in the moonlight flew to the cliff's edge. I was fearful for what I might see, but knew that I had to look. I leaned over to look down at the jagged rocks and fierce waters.

At first, I saw nothing but white sprays of water. But as I turned to leave the cliff's border, a red streak sliced through the darkness. I swiftly focused my attention back on the water. I peered down the cliff. A beam of moonlight struck a small rock in the water.

Next to the solemn rock, red material floated to the surface.

With deliberate cautiousness, I followed the slope of the cliff down toward the raging water. Once the green grass of the slope turned to rock, my high heels became unsuitable for the occasion. With a fast and fluent motion, I removed my heels and placed them to the side. I could feel each black rock jab into the soles of my feet as I continued my descent. I did not slow down.

Right before I reached the water's edge, I noticed that the wet rocks formed a rugged path that twisted back under the castle. At the end of this path is where I had spotted the red cloth. While I was fixated on what was ahead, my foot slipped, and a rock grazed my left ankle. A quick jolt of pain ran through my leg. I briefly applied pressure to the small puncture and then leapt back to my feet. I had to keep going. It felt so slow, much like my dream, as I pushed my way to my goal. I tripped over several more rocks, scraping my hands, elbows, and knees. But I did not stop. Now that I was on a path partially submerged in water, I could feel the sprays dampen my dress. Each splash left my skin with a chill and a deposit of grainy salt.

As the water's hiss grew louder and the moonlight dimmer, I leaned in close to the wall of the cliff to keep my balance. A large wave crashed into my back—I was now completely soaked. Since I had arrived at the water, the rage of the ocean had grown. If I didn't pick up my pace soon, I would be swept into the ocean. I released my grasp on the side of the cliff, brushed the tangles of wet hair from my face, and then leapt to the next heap of rock. Immediately after my successful landing, I leapt again, then again, and again. Each landing was followed with a painful puncture to my heels. Finally, there was only one jump to the exact spot where the cloak had surfaced. I heaved my weight forward and landed in a crouched position on the surface of the rock.

The mound was still encircled with a small light from the moon. I looked down into the shifting water. There was nothing. I shot a panicky glace to my left and right, searching. Nothing. With my legs still bent, I sprung my weight to an upright position to study the area.

Dark, eerie clouds passed in front of the moon, turning the busy sea into a shadowed abyss. If it were any other time, the darkness wouldn't have bothered me, but given the setting and the circumstance, I was more than frightened. I instantly tugged the flap of my bag open and jammed my free hand toward the bottom. After a few seconds of digging, my hand stopped on the rough metal of my flashlight. I swiftly pulled the flashlight out and clicked it on.

A bright line of fluorescent light exuded from the cylinder and illuminated the surface of the water. Using the new ray of light, I investigated the fearsome water again. As the light passed over the patch of sea closest to the rock, I caught a glimpse of something below the surface. The beam of light wiggled. I tried to steady my hand as I peered into the murky water, but my nerves would not allow for it. I shivered at the thought of there being something, or someone, beneath the angry waves. Obviously, this was the reason for my descent, but I had never expected to find anything. The waves continued to crash while I sank back into the mound to take a closer look. I scanned the water slowly, tentatively.

I noticed a tingle on my skin, a strange tingle. It was like a thousand tiny ants were marching up my legs. I shined the light at my legs, but there was nothing on my skin. The tingling sensation moved to my arms—then I felt it on my neck.

Something was happening. I stood up to back away from the water, but was instantly pushed down to my knees. It felt like a wave of air pushing me, but I knew that it couldn't be. The flashlight was shaking in my hand again. Another force came from behind, pushing my head closer to the water. I wanted to cry out, but I knew it wouldn't do me any good. The tingle in my neck became painful as I was forced to stare down into the ocean.

My reflection was there, in the water. I couldn't see it clearly, but it was there. Suddenly, I fell through my reflection; I was in the water. The salt water stung my eyes—I couldn't tell if I was swimming up or down, left or right. At first I was drowning, and then in seconds, I resurfaced inside the mouth of a cave.

-12-

THE CAVE

I SPAT THE REMAINS OF THE OCEAN FROM MY MOUTH AS I LAY on the cool black stones that carpeted the entrance of the cave. It felt therapeutic to suck in the night air. The next thing I was conscious of was the water rising through the opening. I planned to give myself a few moments to catch a good breath, and then I would swim back through the entrance. I didn't want to stay in the clammy cavern any longer than I had to.

Just as I lifted my head from the stones, there was a shuffling of rocks coming from the depths of the darkness. I jumped to my feet, foolishly jittery, holding my flashlight close to my chest. There was something in the cave. This would probably be a good time to exit. I steadily pushed my way into the cold water until the swells met my waist. I took a few deep breaths and readied myself for the dive.

As I took my last profound breath, I heard a soft giggle resonate in the darkness. The hair stood up on my arms, while I held my breath. *It's not real... There is no rational explanation for this.* I pushed the air from my lungs so that I could speedily take another. I was more than ready to leave this place.

Then, right before I dove into the water, I heard something that sent a shiver over my skin—one simple word.

"Stop." The voice was from a young girl. Her soft cry echoed through the night air.

I was not alone. I stood there with my back to the darkness and questioned what I should do. *Is this the girl I saw fall from the cliff?* If she was down here, I sure couldn't leave her to drown.

"Wait." The voice pleaded again.

This time I turned to direct a beam of light toward the voice. The light bounced off a red cloak darting further into the cave. I attempted to move toward her quickly, but the water made my feet heavy and slow to move. After a good minute of struggling, I made it to the water's edge, exactly where the moonlight ended. My flashlight was now my only source of light. The cool, stale air filled my lungs as I took off running into the belly of the cave.

When I came to the place where the girl had been standing, I noticed the walls of the cave took a sharp left and tunneled to a lower elevation. I paused to shine the light down the tunnel and saw nothing but the fancy rock sculptures created by the timeless power of the sea.

I turned back to examine the rise of the water coming from the entrance. The tide was rising very quickly; it wouldn't be long before the entire entrance would be underwater. I had to find this girl soon so we could swim out before the waves filled the tunnels. I looked back to the belly of the cave and then dashed into the unknown.

The cave took one dramatic turn after the next and narrowed each time. I had no time to hesitate—I simply ran down each slippery, dark tunnel. In my mind I made a mental layout of what I had passed to prevent later confusion.

I finally came to a seemingly dead end. There was a tunnel, but this tunnel was not like the others. At a glance, it looked like a dark shadow in the far corner of the wall, but as I stepped closer with the flashlight, I could see that it was more than a shadow.

I dropped to my knees and shined the light down into the small opening, hoping that it didn't lead to anything. Hoping that I wouldn't have to go through it. Just as I extended my arm with the flashlight, I saw the girl with the red cloak. She was in the tunnel. I would have to crawl.

The tunnel was much too small for comfort, but I had to go in. I had to help the girl. I shifted my shoulders and pushed my weight through the narrow lips in the wall.

"Where are you going?" I asked with a stern tone. My voice bounced from the walls.

The girl continued to slide down further into the darkness. She made it quite clear that she had no desire to stop, but I was not leaving without her. I had almost caught up with her, when the girl abruptly dropped out of sight. The tunnel had opened into a large chamber. I fell out of the tunnel, right after her, and took a few seconds to scan the new room with the light.

The chamber was perfectly round and decorated with hundreds of rock formations glistening with beads of water. I shined the light upward to the ceiling, but the light faded into a dark, circular shadow. We were standing in the bottom of a giant tunnel.

Water began to hiss and crash into the room. I directed my attention and flashlight back to the girl, and for the first time, I could see her face clearly.

Her skin was the perfect shade of ivory, and her rosy cheeks and lips gave her the appearance of a china doll. I watched in silence as she looked up into the emptiness of the chamber and closed her eyes. Her red cloak finally relaxed against her white nightgown as she stood completely still in this position.

"We must go," I said gently this time.

She did not move. I walked toward her while the cold water gushed in through the tunnel to cover the floor. She swiftly dropped her head down and opened her eyes to meet my gaze.

"Stop," she commanded.

My heart jumped. There was something about her voice that startled me.

"Where are you going?" she questioned.

I took a step back in the rising water. Her small rosy lips had moved, but it was my own voice that escaped her mouth.

With the light still shining on her porcelain face, I watched as her lips moved with mine when I muttered, "I'm going home."

I frantically took another step back, but stumbled, and dropped the flashlight. Without thought, I snatched the light and pointed it back to the girl. She was gone. My eyes scanned the perimeter of the chamber. There was no sign of her. The water was now knee-deep and surging in faster with each second. My mind swirled, trying to wrap itself around an explanation, but I could think of none. I looked carefully through the chamber, looking for anything to explain what I had just witnessed. The girl was nowhere to be found. She had simply disappeared into the dark. By this time the water had doubled to be waist-level. I had to go. I turned and began to make my way back to the opening.

As I waded in the dark, cold water, I took one last glance back into the chamber. Only darkness stared back. The rage of the water pushed against my legs with great force as I neared the entrance to the narrow tunnel. I aimed the flashlight down the eerie passageway to observe the speed of the incoming water. My heart fluttered with panic as I watched it crash against the sides of the rocky path. It looked like a tunnel from a water park, except less friendly.

There was no doubt in my mind that this chamber would soon be completely filled. And with the increasing force of the water, I couldn't crawl back through. My only chance of survival was to keep my head above the water and float up the tunnel of the chamber.

I shivered as the water splashed to my chest, and took short and frequent breaths as my nerves began to take over. I knew that I had to act quickly. With the strap of my bag, I looped the slack around the handle of my flashlight until it formed a tight knot. Once the water rose, I would need to use my arms to swim.

Soon after I secured the light, a loud roar escaped the small, narrow tunnel. I shuddered at the thought that I could possibly be meeting my death. Another rattling roar escaped. I tried to keep my weight balanced as the bottom of my feet lifted from the slippery surface of the cave floor. It was evident that I was being hurried up the tunnel in a spinning movement. In seconds the water had pushed my body through the dark shadows of the chamber's ceiling. And from the sound of the water, I was convinced that my ride had only begun.

After I realized that the force of the water would keep me afloat, I tucked my legs under my body and lifted one arm to the surface as a precaution to shield my body from the walls. I ascended into a pitch-black tunnel. The old smell of moistened rock was now overpowered by a much stronger smell of sweetness. The undeniable smell reminded me of the honeysuckles and gardenias that used to take over our backyard every summer. I wished I were home now.

My thoughts were unexpectedly interrupted with an odd bubbling sound from below. The bubbles tickled as they floated under my feet, through my legs, and around my arms to burst at the rough surface. The flashlight that had been hanging from the strap of my satchel illuminated the growing number of bubbles.

Vivid lights began to penetrate the water as I was hurled upward.

-13-

PINE LIGHT

My eyes flickered open to a cloudy night. The moon looked huge in the sky, resting close to the water—it felt almost too close. I rolled to my feet and then shuffled up a sandy hill until it met with grass. I expected to see light pouring from the rose-colored panes of Scarlet Heights, but what I saw was something different entirely. What I saw was *pine light.*

It was strange at first—almost frightening. But then it was magically beautiful. A thick forest covered the land for as far as I could see. The trees of the forest flickered and swayed as if they were dancing with sparklers to the wind's melody. Pine light. I walked softly in the velvety grass in the direction of the sparkling forest. I stepped among the trees and stood frozen in awe as the cool, sweet air blew through my hair and around my face. As the wind quickened, the brown pine needles from the elder trees came alive with a sudden, colorful glow. The wind caught the flickering needles and gracefully carried them to the ground as they faded back to their original color. I was left breathless from the light display.

Is this a dream? Am I dead? I wasn't sure. As my eyes wandered to the belly of the woods, I noticed that pine needles twinkled from every tree. The random bursts of illumination added to the list of questions that had been running through my restless mind. I needed answers. I decided to push forward into the unknown.

I walked for hours, carefully observing my surroundings. The trees still were swaying, but the wind had turned their soft dance into a vigorous shake. Nevertheless, the bright pine needles continued their float down to the floor of the forest.

As I weaved through the tall shadows and tree trunks, I found a small clearing with a single tree. In this area there were no shrubs, just a bent-over tree with green grass and fading pine needles beneath it. It seemed as if the tree, which shadowed this small place, was inviting me in to rest. I graciously accepted the invitation by dropping my bag on the ground and positioning my head on its roots while extending my legs over the soft grass.

While resting, I studied the woods that had captivated me hours before. Faded pine needles lay all around, carpeting the floor of the entire forest. I automatically reached for the nearest cluster. My fingers slid over the pine needles, igniting the cluster with a brilliant ray of sparkling light. Stunned, I dropped the inexplicable needles. At this point, I was confused beyond reason. With my body still resting against the bark, I reached to my right side and grabbed a whole handful of pine clusters. Just like the first cluster, they all began to glow. I slid my thumb and index finger along the edge of the needles. They felt warm, as if they had been bathing in the sun all day.

I grabbed for my bag, carefully placing the pine needles between my dead flashlight and the book of poems. My attention fell to the gift that Fergus had given me. It was still wrapped in a dusty cloth—still a mystery.

While my eyes gazed up at the tree, I could only think of what Fergus had told me. I rolled to my side and placed the fabric on the ground in front of me. And as my hand traced the edges of the wool, my mind began to replay bits and pieces of the stories that Fergus once told.

His stories had constantly intrigued me. I would spend hours in the library, listening to his every word. They would always begin blissfully and somehow lead to a dark and twisted tale with characters fighting for their lives and their beliefs. He would tell them with such great detail that they had a sense of realness. There had been times when I had felt like I could see everything he described as if I were there. A mild wind swept through the trees and blew my hair into my eyes. With one finger I slid the hair back into place and then reached for the brown fabric. I wanted to know everything there was to know. I gently unfolded the fabric.

Underneath the flap of wool lay a beautiful cross.

I ran my fingers over the aged necklace, carefully inspecting the front and the back. The metal cross in my hand was the same as the one I had seen in the book from the dream. Pine needles wound around the center of the cross, forming the Trinity. The needles lit up as I ran my fingers around the endless knot. The cross was breathtaking in person. As I sat the cross down on the wool, the pine needles returned to their dull state of rest. A thin ribbon wound through the top of the cross, forming a necklace. The fiber, which was similar to twine, had been torn at the ends. An easy fix, but noteworthy nonetheless. I carefully placed the cross on my neck and reached behind to knot the fiber necklace. I could feel warmth radiating from the cross as it fell to my chest.

I lay there in the woods, gazing down at the cross, until I noticed a drastic change in the weather. The nice cool breeze that had once swept through my hair was now a strong gust blowing dramatically through the trees from all directions. I had an uneasy feeling in the pit of my stomach. The wind felt much like a warning, almost as if it were trying to tell me a storm was on its way and to seek shelter. I could smell a hint of rain and ash blowing through the trees, eliminating the sweet perfume of the pines. The soft light in the woods grew dimmer by the minute. I needed to find a safe place soon.

I heard the faint sound of branches snapping behind me as I lifted myself from the trunk of the tree. I turned to investigate, but could see nothing in the poor lighting. I grabbed my bag and took to walking. My attention quickly darted above when I heard a loud rumble coming from the sky. Just as I looked up, the sun was blocked by dark blue clouds, which now covered the entire sky. The once bright and cloudless sky looked like a wild sea of deep blue and black, angry clouds. I felt a prickly slap on the back of my shoulder and turned in time to see the branches of the trees slapping vigorously at me. It felt as if the forest was alive and trying to get me to move forward. I heard another snap. This time the noise was much closer in the woods behind me.

An unnerving feeling began to pulse through my veins. I wasn't the only one out here. Something or someone was watching me. I shifted my body to the right and pressed my back to a tree trunk that was twice my size in width. I heard a sound again. This time it sounded much like rustling in the brush, followed by a low-pitched mumble. I felt my heart pound, almost as if it were trying to escape my body. The pounding made each breath painful.

A single drop of rain hit like a glass bead on the top of my head. I did not move as it rolled down over my forehead and into my eye. I could feel the bark of the tree leaving its impression on the skin of my back as I tried to disappear into its wide trunk. I listened with all of my strength, waiting to hear another noise coming from behind. All I could hear now was the sound of the wind raging to the frantic beat of my own heart. I knew that I could not stay behind the tree all night, so I reluctantly decided to peek around the trunk. If I did not spot anything, then I would make a run for it.

I gradually turned my body to the right so that my side and cheek rested on the warm bark. Before I could tilt my head forward, I felt a sharp pinch on the exposed side of my neck. The spot tingled. As I reached for my neck, my hand landed on something else.

Protruding from my skin was a short, pencil-like object. Without hesitation, I applied pressure to my neck with one hand and pulled the hard tube out with the other. I could feel my skin tear as my whole neck began throb with a sharp pain. I held the object tight as my body began to slide down the side of the tree. Once I was flat against the ground and tree, I opened my hand to observe what had caused my injury. In my hand lay a clear dart, no longer than three inches. One end of this device was a tiny white fluff of feathers, while the other end came to a sharp needle point. In frustration, I jabbed the lightweight dart into the ground. Someone was out there, and they were after me.

I tried to pull my weight back up, but my legs were weak. I noticed that I could not hear the wind anymore, just a soft ringing in both of my ears. Then complete silence. My mouth felt dry, and everything looked blurry and spotted.

In my peripheral vision, I made out shadows to my left and right. Though afraid beyond explanation, my heart was no longer racing, but gradually pounding slower and slower. I allowed my body to fall forward into the soft ground and attempted to pull my weight with my hands and elbows. My knees shook while I pushed them into the earth. I had only crawled a few feet when my entire body turned cold. Then everything faded to black.

-14-

PIRATES

It was dark when I gained consciousness, and I was soaked to the bone. My pounding head rested facedown on what I imagined to be damp rope. I squirmed. My hands were bound behind my back, and my feet were tied and jammed between two heavy, round objects. I was helpless, again. Warm blood pumped through my cold veins to the tear in my pulsing neck. My feet and hands were still frozen and tingling. I was afraid. I never feared death, only the thought that it would be introduced with hellish pain. So in these moments of waking up, I only feared that I would soon experience unbearable pain.

I had to get loose. I shifted my stiff shoulders back and forth several times to push the twisted rope out from under my head. I did the same with my hips and knees, until the rope was no longer underneath my body. I was now lying flat on my stomach against a rough surface, but I felt as if my body was still rocking back and forth. I twisted my bound feet upward so that I was free to rest on my back. I felt the surface of the floor—it was hard, cold, and wet. I could feel tiny cracks and ridges between miniature pools of water. A small prick to my index finger suggested that the surface was wooden. The floor jolted. My muscles tensed as I tried to keep my body from rolling. There was a faint sound of footsteps from above. Another jolt. This time I couldn't keep my body from rolling to its side. I pressed my ear against the grains of the wood floor and shut my eyes, trying my hardest to focus on capturing another sound. For a moment I heard nothing, but then out of the silence came a roar and a hiss of water knocking its way against my wooden prison. I ran my tongue against my lips and felt the grainy texture and taste of salt left on my skin by the sea. The thought of being imprisoned on a ship filled my mind with terror.

"Everything will be okay…" I murmured to myself. Footsteps interrupted my thoughts again, but this time they were much louder. All I could do now was remind myself to breathe. So I took a breath, then exhaled…then took another…and exhaled…and on the third breath, a wooden door that had been hidden in the darkness flew open.

I was expecting a rush of light to enter, but instead was surrounded by a moist wind filled with the smell of salt, fish, and sweat. Only the flickering light of a lantern, held tightly by a small, aged man. lit the entrance to my cell.

He took a few steps into the room and paused while a much larger and frightening man made his way through the door. Both men stomped in wearing tall, rugged black boots. The dim light was now close enough for me to make out the coil of rope I had wrestled with and the two heavy barrels that had trapped my feet. I still couldn't make out any of the other shadows in the room.

As the two men made their way closer, they seemed to study me as I was studying them. The smaller of the two wore baggy brown clothing. His long-sleeved shirt, which was much too big, was ripped halfway down the middle and covered in dark stains. His pants matched with similar stains and holes down the side. The only other color he wore was a rusty sash, which tied around his waist, holding a large scroll of paper to his side. His skin appeared as leather around his forehead and chin. The sun had definitely damaged his youth ages ago. He held the lantern a little higher and motioned with a nod to the larger man. As he nodded, I could see his long, stringy gray hair swaying against his shoulders in the small breeze that was still pushing its way through the door. With the new position of the lantern, I could see more of the second man. He was several feet taller than the man holding the lantern. He stood with his shoulders back, as if he were proud. Even with a mere flicker of light, you could see his chiseled shoulders and arms through his beige shirt. His shirt, though torn and dirty, was much cleaner than the older man's shirt. He was wise in choosing a darker brown for his pants, leaving only the holes noticeable.

He calmly stepped toward the lantern as the older man, seemingly impressed, asked, "This is the catch from yesterday?"

With a hint of a grin, the built man flexed and assertively replied, "I got this one myself…I think he will be pleased."

I immediately began to push against the barrels with my joined feet in an effort to create more distance between myself, and the very man who had put me in this place.

"Well, well…you're lively." The older man chuckled. He held his lantern high and squinted in my direction. "She doesn't look like the others. You best take her to the Cap'in, see if he wants her with the others."

As he turned to leave, I pushed my upper body forward with my tied arms and cried, "Wait!"

He stopped and slightly turned his head back to glance. I had his attention for a moment, so I thought I would ask the obvious. "Why am I here?" I forced the words out loudly, so that the quiver in my voice might go undetected. Neither of the men moved nor said a word.

The aged man smiled a very crooked and dirty smile, then turned and walked to the door. He paused long enough to hang the lantern on a hidden hook. The small flicker of flame cast a small glow of light that faded before reaching the bottom of my feet. The larger man was nothing more than a shadow to me now.

Before I could say another word, the shadow pushed the two heavy barrels apart from my feet as if they weighed nothing. I did not move as I felt him tug at the ropes that had my feet fastened together. As soon as he pulled the last loop of the rope free from my feet, I frantically began to kick upward. I knew that this might be my only chance to break free from of my captor, so I was determined to make the best of the moment. Luckily, I felt my right heel plunge into the side of the shadow's nose and heard a grunt escape from the man. I immediately pulled my freed legs underneath my body and, by using my knees and elbows, managed to stand. Before I took a single step, the man from the shadow reached out and grabbed a handful of my hair. I could feel pain coming from my scalp, but I did not scream. He pulled me backward by my hair until he was close enough to grab my neck. The pain from my scalp did not let up as he squeezed harder and harder at my throat. I felt sharp pain shooting up the side of my neck where the dart had been, while my airway was slowly beginning to shut. As he forced my body to the floor, splinters of wood pierced into my elbows and thighs. He pushed his body toward mine and glared with his black eyes.

"I will teach you to behave," he growled.

Tears were beginning to form in my eyes from lack of oxygen, but I was trying my best to hold them in. He released his grip from my neck only to grab my hair again. With his free hand, he reached around his waistband and pulled out a large knife. I could feel my heart thumping against my chest in fear. He jerked my hair to force my head back to the floor again and placed the knife over my exposed neck. As the sharp blade pressed into my skin, I couldn't help but feel hopeless. With one quick motion, he raised the knife from my neck and sliced through the hair that he had gripped in his hand. His lips formed a devilish grin once he threw the hair to my side. Warm streams of tears fell from my eyes and rolled down each side of my face. I tried to lift my head, but he grabbed another handful of hair and cut it off. All I could do was watch as he threw more and more hair to my side. After he was satisfied with his work, he slid his knife back into his waistband and stood up.

"Do not test me again," he said as he grabbed my bound arms. He pointed to the large pile of wavy brown locks that used to be mine and said in a stern voice, "This is so you won't forget."

In a sequence of effortless motions, he grabbed my arm, pulled me back to my feet, and then threw me over his shoulder. I did not fight back this time. I watched through tear-filled eyes as he carried me through the room, up several narrow steps, to the bridge of the ship. I looked behind us—nothing but barrels of potatoes, buckets of rags, and woolen sacks were behind us.

I gasped when we surfaced.

The magnitude of the ship was overwhelming. Long, darkened boards ran straight across the deck—scuffed and knotted with age. Waves as big as thirty feet flew over the sides, tossing the vessel and coating the deck with salt water. The sea was angry.

I had never been out to sea. Now I was out to sea on a ship—kidnapped by pirates. If I hadn't been scared to death, I would have been fascinated beyond belief. Everything I had experienced in the last forty-eight hours had been surreal. I was still trying to process the idea of vampyres—or fallen angels—and now I had to add pirates to the list?

We plunged forward through an almost gale-force wind that encircled the deck of the ship, carrying enormous drops of icy rain. I could feel the wind and rain combing its way through my newly shortened hair as I was lugged across the deck to the cabin of the ship. Ropes appeared to dangle from the sky. Shadows were in the darkness—shadows of dingy, rugged men running about the deck, pulling and tightening the ropes hanging from the large sails.

As we approached the cabin, a large wave of ocean swept over the right side of the ship, drenching the remainder of my damp clothes. It was with this rush of cold water that the last flicker of flame in the lantern was smothered. My captor angrily chucked the lantern to the deck floor and then reached for the door.

A small wave of warmth and light escaped through the opening as the door creaked open. I noticed a fireplace with a mantel in the front portion of the room. The heat from the fireplace was comforting as it seeped through my skin to warm my bones. I felt my weight shift—my captor dropped me to the floor. I landed with a hard thud on my hip next to a large desk and chair. Before I could let out much of a whimper, he reached down and retied the rope around my hands so that it looped one of the long legs of the desk.

"Do not move," he said as he slipped his way back out of the cabin.

The cabin was comfortable compared to the bottom deck, and there was much more to take in. Over the fireplace, on the ledge of the dark brown mantel, were a variety of scrolls and rusty lanterns. The scrolls were similar to the one that had been tucked around the waist of the older man who had studied me before. Above the mantel was an old, faded map. It didn't look like any world map I had ever seen. I squinted, trying to make out the shapes and words.

A man entered the cabin. He was tall, more slender than the man who had dragged me from the lower quarter of the ship, but looked just as tough. His personal hygiene was not lacking, and his dress code was much sharper than that of the crew. He wore a stereotypical tricorn hat, a rich wine-colored waistcoat, knee breeches, and bucket-topped boots—I could only assume he was the captain.

"They told me you were different than the other females." I scooted back as far as the desk would allow, while he knelt down to touch my torn dress. He acted confused by my clothing—or mesmerized by the material. I couldn't quite tell.

"What land are you from?" he asked.

"What's it to you?" I snapped. I wasn't sure where the rush of courage had come from.

"I can do dreadful things to you, if I so choose—things you wouldn't imagine. It's in your best interest to answer me."

"Ireland," I said quickly. "I came from Ireland."

"Ire Land? There is no such place."

"Yeah. There is."

"I have sailed these seas a hundred years over. There is no land by that name." He glared back at me—my certainty had piqued his interest. He grabbed my arm and yanked me over to the map above the mantel. "Show me. Show me where this land is."

A hundred years over? That would be impossible; the man couldn't be a day over forty. I scanned my eyes over the map.

"It's-It's…" It wasn't there. I didn't recognize anything. The majority of the map was water and marked *the Deltic, Northern, and Relik Oceans.* And there were three large pieces of land, Zy, Everest, Kenya—they were laid out like a triangle in the water. Islands of different shapes and sizes were sprinkled inside the triangle, while a few surrounded them. I didn't recognize a single name on the map, and I could have sworn I saw something marked *The Devil's Backbone.*

The man who had threatened me before barged into the cabin.

"Cap'in—we have a stowaway on board."

"A stowaway? On my ship?"

"Yes, Cap'in."

"Throw the rodent overboard."

"W-We haven't found him yet, sir."

"Can you imbeciles do nothing?"

He shoved me over to the man. "Put her with the others. Make sure the ropes are tied tight, and weigh down her feet. I'm warning you, Hayes—if she gets loose, it's your neck."

As soon as the captain left, I was forced back into the rain. This time, instead of being escorted into a warm cabin, I was thrown under the deck of the ship.

It smelled down there. Smelled of dirt and sweat and many horrible things. A group of girls who were tied and gagged huddled in a corner when we entered. I was tied to a rope that bound all of us together, gagged with a rag that smelled like kerosene, and then my ankles were wrapped with a heavy chain. Before leaving, the man pushed me to the floor, knocking over all of us like bowling pins. He laughed his way out of our prison.

This was the longest night in my life. My stomach churned and growled for food;my lips craved water. I tried to close my eyes—to pretend this was all a nightmare—but it was useless. The ship rocked us back and forth, pushing us into one another. The girls moaned through their gags, sharing in the same feeling of helplessness. We were their victims, and there was nothing we could do about it.

The next day we were pulled from the pit for another kind of torture. The captain ordered that we were to be cleaned for presentation. One by one we were separated from the group, and a thick rope was tied around our waist. Then we were forced to watch as each girl was lowered over the side of the ship and dunked into the ocean. It was terrible to watch, especially the younger ones. They cried in terror, hoping that they would be pulled from the water in time to breathe. I was the sixth girl to go, and it was all I could do not to scream. But then it was over, and we were tied back together.

We were ordered to stand along the edge of the ship and remain standing unless we wanted to be thrown back into the ocean for another dunk. No one moved.

A few hours later, when the sun was high in the sky, land appeared on the horizon. The land became closer and closer over the next hour. Before long we seemed to be right on it. The ship followed the high, rocky coastline, until it came to an opening in the rock. It was a cave of some sort, large enough for two vessels. This is where the ship dropped its anchor.

The crew herded us all into a small boat, lowered it down into the blue water, and began to paddle into the dark cave. Several boats followed with the rest of the crew and the captain. All of us huddled in silence, scared that this was the end of the road, scared we were about to meet our death in the belly of the cave.

-15-

MASKED ANGEL

"BRING THEM TO ME." A BOOMING VOICE RESONATED FROM the back of the enclosure. My eyes scanned the new environment, looking for the man behind the voice. Dozens of candles lined the walls of the cave, lighting our path. But no man was in sight.

Soon the air grew stale, as if it had been locked away in a glass jar for years. Every breath smelled of smoke and moldy air. My lungs burned for the first few minutes of taking in the awful air. I limited my breathing to the bare minimum, in fear that the air held some kind of past sin.

The men from the crew gnarled their sweaty faces as they watched us step from the boat onto the dark and wet sand. In a matter of minutes, we were out of the water and herded into a circle. I felt the rope tighten as the smaller and frightened girls darted behind me. I tried to stand my ground without showing signs of my fear.

"Everything is going to be all right," I muttered to myself a few times and then turned to whisper to the small, shivering girls behind me. Just as I turned my attention back to the dark, a man dressed in black came out of the shadows.

His posture was perfect and his stride graceful. As he neared, he lifted his head to reveal a perfectly sculpted porcelain mask. The mask was chiseled to a stern, yet elegant facial expression. It was beautiful—one could only imagine that the face underneath matched its beauty. The crew ceased their cursing and lowered their heads as he approached their captain. A deafening silence took over the cave.

The mystery man did not greet them.

"You are late." His voice was strong and somehow alluring at the same time.

"We got in a bit of bad weather," replied the captain. "My greatest apology to you, sir." The captain's voice trailed off as he met the gaze of the mystery man. The masked man seemed irritated, but more interested in the group of us huddled together than the captain.

As he approached our group, I stood completely still with my head tilted slightly down. The man gracefully circled the group, inspecting each girl with his darting eyes. I watched his boots go in and out of focus, until they abruptly stopped on the ground that held my stare. I did not move while the boots stepped forward. The man in the mask tenderly placed his hand under my chin and lifted my head until our eyes met. His deep brown eyes seemed to glow with a piercing green as he looked into mine. At first, my mind told me I should be terrified, but while our eyes were locked, I felt a part of him—a deep emotion, a deep connection to him. I could only see and hear him in those moments. I had forgotten how I came to be here—nothing else existed, nor mattered.

His eyes glanced to my lips. "What is your name?" He beautifully articulated each word and then softly swept the hair away from my eyes. The cool leather from his glove felt refreshing against my newly flushed skin.

"Clara." My response seemed uncertain in the silence. I took a short breath. "My name is…" His fingers silenced my words before they could take flight.

He met my gaze again and softly whispered, "Clarabella." It sounded as though he was smiling.

While the moments passed, I desperately desired to touch the smooth, flawless skin surrounding his mask. I imagined that the face underneath the motionless porcelain was a flawless work of art. My thoughts caused my heart to race, and I knew that he could sense it. I held my breath to slow the beating down as he gently stroked what was left of my hair.

As he examined my condition, his lips tightened and he gripped his cold black gloves into a fist. I immediately felt uneasy with his sudden change of gestures. My thoughts were interrupted when he swiftly turned and made his way to the crew. He continued to rub his hands together, clenching and unclenching his fists, as he neared the captain.

"Tell me," he said as he paced back and forth around the men. "Who among you is responsible for the injuries placed upon this young lady?"

He glanced away from the captain long enough to elegantly point in my direction. He had asked as if he were genuinely concerned about my care while in their possession. The masked man stepped forward to place himself directly in front of the captain and rested one of his gloved hands on the man's quivering shoulder.

"Do not make me inquire again," he said sternly.

The captain shouted, "Hayes…It was my quartermaster, Hayes, that is responsible."

The masked man quickly drew his attention to the man I had feared the entire voyage. My captor had been standing behind two smaller members of the crew; he did not stand as proud as he once did before. The black frock coat of the mystery man seemed to float past the other members of the crew to the accused. From beneath the sculpted mask, he commanded the man to step forward.

The entire crew, including the captain, became painfully still while they watched Hayes push his way to the front. Although the majority of the mystery man's face was covered, I could make out an expression of anger from the skin surrounding the edges of the porcelain mask. The mask leaned forward so that it almost touched the face of the man who had once dominated me with such ease.

"Is this indeed the truth?"

Hayes timidly nodded while staring into the mask.

"Are you also the man who cut her locks of hair?"

I caught a tremble as the man responded with a hesitant "aye."

In one rapid motion, the masked man's sword was no longer by his side, but in his hand. "May you never make that mistake again!"

The coattail of my defender swayed as he thrust the end of his sword into the chest of the man called Hayes. He defeated him as he forced the sword through his entire body. I gasped for air as I watched him fall to his knees in agony. The man behind the mask pulled the sword from his victim in time for him to fall face-forward into the ground. Blood spilled from the man's body and soaked into the sand, until he was completely encircled by a red flowing river. I'd never seen so much blood. A sick feeling came over me as I realized I had just witnessed the death of a man.

The rope that wrapped around my wrists and the other girls' twitched and tightened as the girls pulled away in fear. The cave became silent again, and all I could hear was the slow pounding in my ears. The nausea turned to a dizzy spell, and I could feel the blood slowing down in my veins. My consciousness was fading into a spotted abyss.

Before my knees had time to buckle, the masked man flew to my side and scooped my body into his arms. In only moments, I was untied from the other girls and gliding through the air. The terror I had felt was pushed away when my head fell against his shoulder.

There was an aura about him that was terrifying and somehow captivating. While my body was pressed to his, I could only feel the beauty. My head continued to spin lightly while I took in his seductive aroma. His cool skin exuded a warm, spicy essence, which was both velvety and narcotic. While I filled my nose with this scent, I could feel the life come back to my body. I felt him pause in front of the captain.

"Leave, now…and take the body with you," he said. No one questioned him.

I felt a light breeze brush against my face when he began to carry me away from the scene and into the dark corner he had entered. Once in the corner, he stopped again.

"See to the other girls." This time he whispered to someone who had been waiting in the dark. I peeked over my shoulder, but I could only see a blurry shadow scurrying in the dark. He took a few more steps, turned, and then leaned into the wall until a door creaked open. A puff of stale air encircled us as he carried me into a slender hallway.

The air was much easier to breathe than the air from the cave, but there was still a faint smell of smoke radiating from the torches hanging on the walls. The hallway was dim, but the torches gave off enough light to see the detail in the man's mask. I lifted my head from his shoulder and stared, daunted by our closeness. He noticed my alertness, and a small grin formed over his enticing lips.

"Who are you?" I questioned very carefully.

He hesitated. "I am who you imagine me to be."

"But what is your name?...I want to know who you are," I said with an unintentional puzzled expression.

He chuckled at my anxious reply. "My actions should show you who I am, not my name." He paused for a moment, allowing the echo of his words to fade into silence. "A name is simply a label that cannot describe, nor explain, who I am. You must understand, Clara...I am no more a name than a name is me."

His answer frustrated me.

"I would like to walk now," I said with an uncompromising tone.

Without a word, he smoothly placed me on my feet and grabbed my wrist. I did not wish to pull away. Even though his face was covered, I could sense that he was bothered by my reaction. I listened to the flame of the torches dance in the air as we passed them one by one. We finally came to a split in the hallway that led into three corridors that were as dark as a moonless night.

Without releasing his grip on my wrist, he grabbed the nearest torch with his free hand and directed us into the opening on the right. The flame of the torch crackled and waved excitedly as we walked further into the gloomy labyrinth. I walked behind him slowly, waiting for the courage to speak to him again. My curiosity finally seized control, leading me to take hold of the hand that held my wrist.

"Wait," I said bravely.

No sooner had the word left my mouth, than he stopped frozen in his tracks. All my agitation melted when he turned to meet my gaze. I reminded myself to hold back my smile, while his gaze grew deeper and deeper. When I blinked, my thoughts flew back to the questions running through my mind.

"Where are you taking me?" I tried my best to sound only curious and not frightened.

He lowered his torch until I could see the flame flickering in his stare. "Somewhere safe," he said with a low and intoxicating tone.

I wanted to hear more. I stepped closer into his gaze to ask the question I had been dying to ask.

"Why do you wear a mask?"

His head tilted, and his eyes wandered to the darkness. "I wear it for protection."

"Protection?" I was surprised by his answer. "Protection from what?"

He released his hand from my wrist to press his palm to his mask. He took a heavy breath as he allowed his fingers to slide along the edges of the porcelain.

"This mask protects my identity from this world and its perceptions. Do not let it frighten you, Clara." He seemed to realize that I was confused by his answer. "You will understand in time."

I remained silent, still lost in his words.

After walking through numerous tunnels—some tall, some short, some wide, some narrow—we finally came to a dead end. *Maybe he made a wrong turn,* I thought. *We were going down the tunnels awfully fast; it would be an easy mistake.* I stood there thinking to myself and watching him forcefully push the end of his fiery torch into the wall. I heard a scraping noise—the wall slowly slid forward.

When we stepped through the opening in the wall, I turned back to see a white stone column slide back into place. We were in a long corridor that was lined with dozens of columns and stained glass windows. *There must be tons of tunnels in this place,* I thought as I admired the designs in the columns and the colors in the glass windows. The man finally released his grip from my wrist as he began to walk toward an enormous arched doorway. I trailed behind without speaking a word.

I followed his flying coattail through the rounded doorway that led to a dining hall. We passed paintings and sculptures of all shapes and sizes as we entered the room, but all of my focus was directed to an elongated table that stood in the middle of the dining hall.

The table was filled with numerous juicy fruits and desserts. All my senses recognized the golden coconut macaroons, plum puffs sprinkled with sugar, roasted chestnuts soaked in honey, steaming rice pudding, and the alluring smell of spicy gingerbread. In between each cooked dessert were large piles of kiwi, strawberries, pineapples, bananas, oranges, and grapes. As I hypnotically walked to the table, I noticed that golden plates and bowls rested at each end of the table, holding the main course.

"I thought you might be hungry." He darted to the end of the table and elegantly slid a tall chair from the table's edge.

His gaze beckoned to me as I walked over to him and sat down on the oversized chair. I shivered from the touch of the cold chair rubbing against my skin. With little movement, he pulled his long jacket off and flung it over my shoulders. Underneath his jacket, he wore an embroidered vest-like shirt that had small black buttons down the front. His eyes stayed locked on me while I observed his unveiled clothing.

"Please, you need to eat." His heels clicked while he strode to the opposite end of the table, where he took his seat.

He was still quiet as he placed a golden goblet to his lips. I looked down at the roasted turkey sitting before me. If it tasted half as good as it smelled, then I was in for a treat. I picked up the fork sitting next to the plate and stabbed a piece of the meat. It was delicious. After I finished the entire portion of turkey, I dove into the rice pudding and then the gingerbread. The food was perfect. The flavors blended flawlessly together, and with each bite a piece of sweetness lingered on my tongue. As I bit into a plum puff, I leaned back into the chair to enjoy one last burst of perfection. I glanced up to catch the masked man twirling his golden goblet while I finished my treat.

"Was everything to your satisfaction?" His voice was rich and sounded pleased.

"It was wonderful. Perfect, actually." Both words failed to describe the sweet and tart tastes that still remained on my tongue. What I had just eaten was like nothing I had ever tasted, so undeniably splendid—superb. Yet, I noticed he hadn't so much as looked at his food. "Are you not eating?"

"I'm afraid these foods have lost their taste—for me," he said solemnly. "But I'm very pleased you were able to enjoy them."

I quickly shot a hand over my mouth to release a much-needed yawn. *Funny how I suddenly feel so tired.*

"I'm not sure how anyone could pass up a meal like this. Everything is so flavorful; I could eat this every day," I said, rubbing my tired eyes.

"Forgive me, you are tired. I should show you to your room."

"No. I'm not tired," I blurted. Even though my eyes felt heavier by the second, I had a strong desire to stay with him—to discover the mystery behind the man.

His body rose from the chair seated at the other end of the table. Before I could stand tall, he had rushed to my side for assistance.

"You need your rest." His voice had been gentle, but his stare serious.

He gently lured me from the chair, back into the foyer of the castle, with ease. It wasn't until my first step onto the spiral staircase that I realized I had taken his suggestion. By that time, I simply couldn't argue.

I inspected the second staircase that twisted beside us while we rose step by step to the third floor. It was easy to imagine a prince and a princess ascending the other staircase, at another time. I must have still been dreaming.

I slid my fingers along the railing as the stairs twisted to meet with a platform. He took a step on to the platform and shuffled to the right. We went through two elegantly carved doors into another hallway. My eyes passed over painting after painting hanging silently on the walls. Knights in armor, shields, spears, everything medieval, decorated in every way.

We passed several passageways and doors before we finally stopped. The man pointed down a short hallway that ended in a bright red door.

"You are free to roam the castle, but this corridor is forbidden."

"Why exactly?" I asked.

He seemed to be searching for the right words, and then he muttered, "It's not safe."

I could tell he was a uneasy about the subject, and I was fighting off sleep with every step, so I let it go. We walked a little further down the hallway, until we came to another door. The wooden door was almost a mahogany color in the light. I pressed my fingers to the carvings and traced over the lines of a large crown that was guarded by two men—one holding a shield, the other a sword. Every door in the castle seemed to tell a story.

"This is where you will be staying," he said, stepping away from the door. "Have pleasant dreams, Clarabella." He slightly bowed and then walked away.

The heavy door pushed open easily, revealing the green decorative interior of the room. I took a step inside. The walls were lined with delicately carved molding, which stretched like ivy all the way to the highest peak in the tall ceiling. A fireplace was on one side of the room, and an oversized, four-post bed on the other—completing the inviting and cozy design.

The room was comfortable. I was comfortable, almost too comfortable, given my new situation. My life had turned upside down in the last few days—or week. I actually didn't know how long I had been gone. But since I had arrived at the castle, since I had met the masked stranger, I felt safe, and I was slowly forgetting about my problems.

Only moments after my head wiggled into the pillow, I fell into a deep sleep.

-16-

ENCHANTED MELODY

In the darkness of my dream, I heard a low voice call to me. *"Clara...Clarabella."* The voice sounded like music. *"Smile for me, my Clara."*

I could feel my body toss on the bed, but my mind wouldn't wake. I vaguely saw a man in the distance of my dream, calling to me. He motioned for me to come to him. *"Leave your thoughts behind."* His words grew softer as I began to wake.

When I opened my eyes, I had a strong urge to get out of bed and away from the dark. I jumped from the tousled sheets and looked around the room until my eyes adjusted. From beyond the walls, I heard music.

The faint sound of a melody floated in the night air. It sounded familiar. I knew the notes, and it was coming from within the castle. I lightly walked to the heavy mahogany doors I had entered earlier that night. A small draft blew over my nightgown as the doors swung open. Sitting on a small wooden chair was a glowing candlestick. I carefully picked up the bronze candlestick and stepped further into the hall.

A small part of me felt like I knew where to go. I followed the sound to the right path of the hall. The hallway was lined with finer things than before—golden candelabras, gothic sculptures, and several portrait paintings. I did not stop to appreciate the art.

The music was like a drug to me, making everything else pointless. Before long, I noticed the walls, ceiling, and the floor of the hall were marked with a smoky gray color. The further I walked, the more I noticed the dark marks. At the end of the corridor, I came to a black wall.

The same smoky gray marks lined the entire wall, covering all traces of its original beauty. Two golden doors stood proudly in the center. A dim flicker of light escaped from beneath them. I quietly placed my candlestick on the floor and pushed on the cold metal doors until there was an opening large enough to squeeze through. The music grew louder.

I entered through a balcony of a room filled with the scent of burning incense and candlelight. I crept to a wooden rail that stood proudly on the balcony's edge, held on tightly, and leaned over to examine the mysterious room.

The floor itself was a work of art. Huge squares of light and dark golden tiles swirled beautifully across the outside edges of the floor. The swirls of tile then crossed and intertwined to the center of the floor, where they created some type of intricate emblem. The lighting was too dim to make out the exact design, but it was enough light to know that it was stunning.

The ceiling stretched to incredible lengths. The walls leading up to the ceiling were painted with elaborate murals of beautiful men and women reaching for the clouds that seemed to float on the ceiling.

And then I saw him.

He stood gracefully stroking the strings of a violin—his eyes fixed on a statue of a majestic owl. The statue was perched on a tall pillar that overlooked the platform where he was standing. The wingspan of the creature stretched its way up to the painted ceiling of the hall and hovered from the platform over its spectator. Even from a distance I could see the great detail in the statue. The carvings in the stone made the feathers appear soft and the eyes appear glowing. I felt as if I could feel a breeze on my skin coming from the wings of the owl and a sharp glare coming from its glowing yellow eyes.

The man continued playing the enchanting melody—the melody that had led me to the hall. He did not break his stare from the frozen-winged creature. I took this opportunity to scan the remainder of the room with my eyes. To the right of me was a winding staircase that twisted down to the ballroom floor. The fourth or fifth step on the staircase was wider, much like an undersized platform. On the platform sat a small pillar where a golden rose and a single candle rested. Matching golden candelabras lined the walls of the entire room

I carefully took soft steps down the curled stairs, toward the man with the violin. When I reached the platform that held the rose and the candle, I saw his head turn, and I stopped.

Dark locks of hair rested against a face covered with a shiny mask, a mirror mask. His eyes held me in a trance, unable to move from the platform, unable to breathe. As I stood there dazed, he softly placed his violin next to the platform and gracefully walked toward me. I had butterflies in my stomach.

He stepped onto the platform and raised a hand over the single candle. The wick instantly sparked to life, along with every candelabrum in the room. I looked down to the rose just in time to see the crisp golden petals soften to a deep red.

He was standing in front of me with his hand held slightly out, reaching for mine. He did not say a word, nor did I.

There was a strange moment of silence while he escorted me to the ballroom floor, and then, like magic, the solemn melody filled the air again. My hands automatically slid over the black leather gloves, into his hands. The surface of the leather was cold, but inviting nonetheless. He pulled me near as our bodies moved to the music.

Suddenly, we were dancing. The room seemed alive as he twirled me around—like a doll lost in his arms. My mind was flying. I felt lost in a world that was between dreams and awake. He moved closer to my body and rested his cheek on mine. His skin felt like a cool rush of air. His lips looked smooth, like the surface of a priceless pearl. My eyes shut as I took in the gentle, but exhilarating fragrance that followed the cold sensation. His face turned, and his smooth lips and cool bursts of air glided over my cheek to my neck. I began to breathe in rhythm with him. His breathing quickened, and so did mine, as he gently lifted his head. I looked up and saw through the mask into startling dark eyes, but as I searched the darkness I became unexpectedly frightened.

While our eyes were still locked, a swirl of green slowly enveloped the darkness in his eyes as he whispered, "Stay with me." His words were enticing. My eyes gradually closed as my mind began to release my worry and fear.

My head felt light and my body heavy, as if I were falling asleep. I quickly opened my eyes to see a ballroom filled with beautiful men and women dancing around us, smiling. The music grew louder and more intoxicating as we glided around the room. My eyes caught a glimpse of a grand orchestra playing, while a woman wearing a mask and red dress began to sing with the most intriguing voice.

Smile for me
And surrender all your fears
Come to me
I will silence all your tears

Feel my love
No more thoughts of loneliness
Take my hand
Forget all your emptiness

Close your eyes
Let yourself fall from the light
Hear my words
Give yourself to this dark night

Stay with me
Stay with me

"Stay with me..." he whispered again. I could only look in his eyes.

The song seemed to speak to my soul. My mind began to focus on the words as we glided around the room.

"I want to see you." I gradually moved my hand to his face and placed my fingers on the hard edge of his mask. Just as the mask slipped from his face, everything went dark.

-17-

ILLUSION

"ARE YOU WELL RESTED?" A GENTLE VOICE SEEPED THROUGH the cracked door in my room. *It's him. The masked man.*

I heaved myself from underneath the sheets and shyly walked over to him. "How'd you know I was awake?" I questioned, pushing the door further open.

"I have a sense for these things." He paused to point with his eyes at a silver tray in his hand. "May I leave you with this?"

I smiled and then stepped back to give him room to enter. A trail of his spicy fragrance filled the room as he briskly made his way to the bed and placed the tray on its surface.

"Fresh fruit," he said as he traced back to where I was standing. "I hope it's to your liking."

"I'm sure it will be."

"Excellent," he said cheerfully. "I also drew your bath. You'll find the room down the hall to the left. There's a wardrobe inside. Help yourself to fresh clothing."

"I don't know what to say, but thank you for your hospitality. You've been more than kind to me. I will never forget it."

"Your happiness is all the gratitude I require," he said. "Please join me in the front foyer after your bath."

He slightly leaned forward, as a respectful gesture, and then exited the room as promptly as he had entered.

The tray contained a ripe collection of all four of my favorite fruits. Mangos, strawberries, pineapples, and bananas—they were the sweetest and juiciest I had ever tasted. I ate every bit of the fruit on the platter before dragging myself down the hall.

I followed the hall as he had instructed, until I saw steam spilling from a cracked metal door. The room was larger than I expected, especially in comparison to the bathroom I was accustomed to, but it was still a tranquil area. Small candles lit a path through the steamy air and led me to the tub. The porcelain bath was completely round, about three feet tall, and was the size of a large kiddie pool. A narrow table stretched across one end holding sponges, a towel, and a bundle of rosemary.

My bag hit the floor with a thump as I wiggled from the torn red dress I had once adored. In moments, my aching body was submerged in warm, rosemary-scented water. After running the sponge over my skin a few times and working the soothing water through my short hair, I pushed back against the smooth tub, thinking, *Who is this man who shows such interest in me? Why has he favored me over the other girls? Can he help me find my way home?*

The longer I sat there, the less concerned I was about going home. But then I thought about Alice; she was still missing. And Fergus and Norma, they would be searching for me. I knew I couldn't stay here long—I knew I had to get back home.

Questions still tossed around in my head, coming and going like Sunday morning traffic, but there was no way to make sense of it alone. I needed to accept that this land was real so that I could focus on finding someone who could tell me how and why I was here. I stepped from the tub, dried off, and wandered through the steam until I found the wardrobe.

It was pushed back in the corner of the room, flat against the ceramic-tiled wall. The wardrobe was tall, with dark carved wood. The carvings almost reminded me of the door to my room, except the images were of mermaids, not guards. I opened the door to reveal dresses of all colors, made from the most luxurious fabric. I ran my hands over the silky material of each dress until I decided on one.

The dress was hunter green, a little low-cut in the front—but not too low to hide the pendant—with a darker green velvet belt that wrapped around the middle. It was floor-length and split right below the belt to reveal a second silver layer to the dress. The wardrobe, of course, had shoes to match. Light silver slip-ons, with just a hint of heel. I felt older as soon as I slipped everything on.

After carefully closing the wardrobe, I made my way into the cool hallway. Candelabras were burning now, highlighting the way. Before I had made it through the doors that led to the foyer, I noticed an oval mirror beside them. I stopped and, for the first time, saw a reflection that I liked.

I'm not sure if it was the dress, the haircut, or the lighting—but whatever it was, it worked for me. The long dress flowed down to the floor, accenting all the right curves. My short hair had dried into small waves, perfectly framing my face. And even though I stood among the long, quivering flickers of the candelabras, my skin looked brighter and flawless.

Excitement swept over me as I pushed open the doors. A breeze ruffled my hair when I stepped onto the stairs. With my hand on the rail, I gradually made my way down into the foyer.

He stood like a statue at the bottom of the stairs—Michelangelo couldn't have crafted a more handsome stone figure. His lips curled upward, and the hard appearance melted to that of an angel. I admired his beauty with every step of my descent. Even though his face was hidden under a mask, I smiled to myself, thinking he might be admiring me as well.

I was anxious and nervous when I took the last step. To be that close to beauty and perfection was intimidating.

"You are a thing of beauty," he said as he offered his arm to me. Blushing, I looped my hand around his offering. "I would like to show you the kingdom, if you feel your energy is restored. I realize you've had a rough journey, but I think fresh air will do you good."

"I'm fine," I insisted, all too ready to see the light of day again. "But I will only go if you give me a name—any name—which I can call you."

"Edmund," he finally murmured. "You can call me Edmund."

The sky was a dull gray, splintered by dark clouds rolling over the sea. Not the bright blue sky I had hoped to see when we exited the castle walls. A strong wind carried the smell of the coming storm in the air, along with a delicate mist. Edmund helped me into a covered carriage strapped to six black horses wearing silver face armor. There was a cloaked coachman patiently sitting on the front of the carriage. This was the first person, besides Edmund, I had seen since my arrival. *Strange, I never saw anyone, not even a single servant.* Pulling the carriage door shut, Edmund motioned to the coachman, and we were off.

The ride was a bit bumpy and definitely awkward. Edmund had opted to sit across from me instead of to my side on the soft bench. It was bumpy because I had room to slide around on the seat. It was awkward because he stared.

I pushed my insecurity back as best as I could and began to talk. This was my common approach to calming my nerves.

"Looks like there's going to be a big storm." I regretted the obvious statement as soon as it left my mouth. I couldn't believe I had brought up the weather. *Lame.*

"The storms in Everest can be fierce this time of year."

Everest. That was on the map in the ship. Zy, Everest, Kenya—Everest was the largest of the lands that made up the triangle.

As the carriage turned away from the edge of the cliff, I caught a sight of the village below the castle. It had been pillaged, no doubt, leaving it with nothing but tainted land and burnt homes.

"What happened here?"

"War," he said, staring out the window. "It will be rebuilt—now that you're here." His voice held a strange certainty, like he knew something that I did not. It was a certainty that shouldn't be questioned. An eerie shiver crept over me, but melted when he looked back. When our eyes locked, I forgot all about my questions and concerns.

Soon we were passing trees that were shaking in the upcoming storm. Though the trees shielded some of the wind, I could feel its force against the boxy carriage. The horses continued to ascend, pulling the coach over more bumpy terrain, until it came to a sudden stop.

"This is what I wanted to show you," Edmund said, grabbing my hand.

"Then by all means."

He helped me out of the carriage, keeping one hand under mine, with the other on my lower back. My skin tingled where his hand touched.

"Take a look," he said softly.

From this bird's-eye view, I could see the entire layout of the castle, including the half-moon walls that protected it. The kingdom stretched for miles and miles beyond that, disappearing into the dark mist of the upcoming rain.

"This is all your land?"

"Everything you see from this point belongs to me."

I stood there for a moment, studying the kingdom while gusts of wind brushed through my hair. Long green blades of grass ruffled all around us. Below was a meadow filled with yellow daisies, glowing through the haze. A trail of tall pines stood proudly at the side of the castle, meeting with the pines behind us. I turned and noticed the forest was green and bright now; it was not dark, as I had seen before.

A sheet of rain abruptly dropped from the sky, bringing my observation of beauty to an end. We jumped back into the carriage and began our descent back to the castle walls. Images came to me suddenly. *Fire. Drowning.* As I looked through the small window of the carriage, I thought I saw the land differently. The grass was dead, replaced with coal-like soil. The daisies had long withered and died. The forest was yet again dreary and dead, like I had perceived on first glance. But this observation only lasted for a fraction of second, before Edmund slipped my hand in his. Then all was forgotten and I saw the beauty in the land once more.

We reentered the kingdom through the front gates. This was my first time to see the courtyard. There were vines growing on every stone statue and along the entire wall. Plants were in need of grooming, fountains in need of cleaning. But when Edmund pointed to them through the window of the carriage, I saw something completely different. I saw blooming flowers around magnificent statues of lions and owls, bushes groomed to a round perfection. I saw sparkling water running through grand fountains.

Did I imagine the whole thing? I wasn't sure.

Then at last, we were back in the castle. I noticed different things, things I didn't see before, as we walked through its halls. Dried leaves rustled about the castle floor; this caught my attention first. When I looked up, the dozens of white columns I had seen before were covered in vines and soot. There were cracks in the walls and torn drapes on the windows, but only for a fleeting moment. Then its beauty appeared again. Everything was rose-colored once more. I shook my head, confused.

"Come this way," Edmund suggested, turning down a different hall.

I hesitated, looking back at the now perfect columns, before shrugging it all away. *It was nothing. Just your imagination.* Then I took after him down the hall.

We walked up a great flight of steps and then turned down another hall and another, until we came to a giant metal door. I drew a long breath when Edmund opened the door, for this was quite a sight. There were books—thousands of books—stacked high on shelves reaching the cathedral-style ceiling. And a wall of glass, possibly the biggest windowpane I had ever seen, was open to view the dark rain joining the vast ocean below.

"I think you might find these books to be quite magical," he said.

"Can I?" I asked eagerly, pointing to the nearest shelf.

"You can do with them what you like. They are for you."

I ran to the shelf, dodging two oversized chairs, to finger through some of the titles. *The Count of Monte Cristo. Moby Dick. Paradise Lost.*

"Clara," he said as he slowly circled the room, "I have matters to attend to this evening and will be gone until dark."

I looked over my shoulder long enough to catch his eyes darting away from me.

"Can I trust you will stay in the castle?

"Of course. Why would I leave?"

His mask slightly moved when a grin formed over his pale lips.

"I take it you like this room then."

"Oh yes."

"Good. You can stay in here as long as you like. There will be food prepared and waiting for you in the dining hall when you are ready."

And that was all he said before leaving me in the company of the books.

After grabbing *The Count of Monte Cristo* from the shelf, I quickly arranged one of the large chairs to face the window and made myself comfortable in its plush material. Time stopped as I pored through the pages. This had always been one of my favorite books, but never had it seemed so real. Halfway through the book, I became exhausted from it all, so I closed my eyes for a rest. It wasn't long before I was met with a dream.

-18-

DARKNESS STIRS

I WAS RUNNING AWAY FROM A SHADOW.

"Let it burn. Let it all burn!" I kept shouting. I ran down a stone hallway, spreading flames.

But then the shadow caught me, pushing me back with a force so strong that I lost my breath. Thick smoke burned my throat as I gasped for air. A low voice echoed from the dark figure before me, but I could not hear him over my own thoughts. *"He's dead. They're all dead."*

My hand tightened around the pendant still wet with his blood, a reminder of all that I'd lost. Fingers wrapped around my neck, but I ignored them. I wanted him to squeeze—I wanted to die, for I would never join them. I felt a pressure in my head, followed by a pain throughout my entire body. He forced me back through an open red door and threw me into a sea of silk sheets. My vision blurred as my own mind began to betray me. I would never be his.

I was yanked from my nightmare so abruptly, it took me a moment to realize it was over. My skin was hot and sticky. My hands were shaking. I had never had this dream before.

Edmund stood over me, looking down through his cold mask. Something about this sent a shiver through my bones.

"You were dreaming."

I nodded, even though it wasn't a question.

"It upset you," he said. "Drink this."

Until now, I hadn't noticed he was standing over me with a jeweled goblet in his hand.

"I'm fine, really."

But he had already pressed the cold rim to my lips.

"What is it?"

"Taste. You will like this."

I took a sip, feeling every bit of the chilled liquid slide down my throat. At first it was sweet. *Is it wine?* I took another sip. *No.* This was spicy. I took another. Now it was tart. And another. Then it was something differently entirely, but I wasn't sure what that was other than pure ecstasy.

Before long, the liquid was gone, and I wanted more.

"How do you feel?"

"Very good. Can I have more?"

"Not right now."

That wasn't what I wanted to hear. I felt like a kid yearning for more candy. I felt like I had to have more, that I wouldn't be able to stop thinking about it until my thirst had been fully quenched.

"Please?" I begged.

"Look at me." He tilted my face so that our eyes met, but for some reason I was having trouble focusing on his. "You've had enough."

It wasn't long after that I felt a little groggy, then delirious. I started to see things—things that I knew were not real. Like the walls moved. And glass was shattering all around. I thought I saw Erik and the redheaded woman looking over me. *Am I drunk?* Then I was levitating in the air, flying down the hall to my room. The room was spinning, but I managed to land in the bed. I needed to close my eyes.

I heard Edmund's voice cut through the buzz. "I am sorry," he whispered. His cool lips pressed hard against mine until I was no longer aware.

In the black abyss I heard him softly say, "Good night, sweet Clarabella. Tomorrow you will be mine."

-19-

MASQUERADE

I SAT UP IN BED, FEELING SOMEWHAT LIGHT-HEADED. FOR THE life of me, I couldn't remember how I had come to be in bed. *How long have I been asleep?* There was a blank space in my mind from the time I was in the library, until now. There was a carriage ride, then the library. That was all. I fell asleep reading. *But didn't I see Edmund after that?* I stretched while trying to recall the night, then stood, feeling defeated.

On my bed was a long silk gown—a white gown, with accents of white teardrop jewels around the front and white lace down the back. Beside the dress lay a delicate pearl hairpin and a silver mask. The mask matched the design of the gown and was just as beautiful. Silver shoes, embroidered with matching teardrops, rested on the floor below it.

A note lay unfolded on the dress.

Please forgive me for not escorting you downstairs.
When you are ready, meet me in the ballroom.
—E

I quickly shuffled out of the green dress from the day before and slipped into the new white gown. The silk dropped over my head and lay perfectly flat against my body. I twirled a few times, feeling the weight of the material dance around me. I traced the beads along the front where they decorated the curves of my chest. The front swooped lower than my last dress, so I had to work to hide the cross pendant, but I eventually managed.

Without the help of a mirror, I twisted the short pieces of hair around my face, pinning one side with the pearl hairpin and leaving the other side loose. Then, after adjusting the silver mask over my eyes and stepping into the Cinderella shoes, I was ready.

I swayed to a somber melody down the halls of the castle until I came to two golden doors. There was something very familiar about the doors, but I was too excited to study them.

The music pulled me in. I stood at the top of the balcony, waiting for Edmund to find me. I was more than nervous standing there alone. My eyes scanned the hundreds of masked men and women dancing across the floor, until stopping on one. But it wasn't Edmund.

He stood alone in the back of the room with a stare pinned on me, like his life depended on it. He wore all black from head to foot, with the exception of the silver pattern on his cape. His mask was not like the others'. It wasn't jeweled or molded. It didn't glitter, and it wasn't decorated with feathers. It was a simple black cloth tied around his head.

I managed to make it down the stairs without so much as tripping—all twenty-five steps. Maybe I could be graceful after all.

The stranger was standing at the bottom of the stairs when I took my last step down. His eyes were piercing through his mask. He quickly took my hand in his and led me through the crowd to the dance floor. I noticed his fingers were warm as they wrapped around my entire hand. He stopped once we reached a small opening and placed his other hand on my lower back. I could only think of him touching me. We stepped into the music.

After a few twirls around the floor, he leaned in to whisper in my ear.

"I don't have much time here, Clara—so listen closely."

"How do you know me?" I tried to sound calm.

"That isn't important. Listen, you must leave this place, Clarabella." He pronounced my name softly and carefully.

I was still staring at him when his enticing eyes darted back to mine. Couples circled around us from every direction, but his eyes were focused only on me. At this point it was comforting to know that my worried expression was behind a mask.

"Why would you say that? I've seen nothing but kindness."

"Listen, you are in danger. Do not trust Edmund." He continued quickly with a concerned tone. "And do not trust what you see. Edmund is the king of deceit and illusion; you will see only what he desires." He spoke with a passion that was hard to ignore.

"Why should I believe anything you say?"

"I wish," he whispered, "I wish you could remember…"

He reached for my face, but I turned my back to him. He quickly placed a hand around my waist, pulled me into his body, and swayed back into the music. I could feel his warm presence behind me, and I could hear the quickening of his breath in my ear. There was nothing but a secret passion in that moment.

In a faint and mesmerizing voice, he began to sing, "Smile for me…and surrender all your fears. Come to me…I will silence all your tears."

While his voice surrounded me with a warm embrace, he loosened his grip from my waist and allowed his fingers to brush against my arms. I marveled at the voice that interrupted my thoughts and caused my heart to flutter. His voice gently faded into the sounds of the orchestra, while his feet shuffled to take a step closer to me.

"There was a time that my words meant something to you," he said tenderly. I felt his breath on the back of my neck, and an appealing rush came over me. "I understand that time has passed, but you must trust me."

"What do you want from me?" I muttered.

"Let your mind imagine." His voice was gentle. "Think of pines and fire…of dark owls from the north. Please imagine it."

His words struck me in a strange way. As he spoke, images flashed in my head. *Fire. Drowning*—the same images I had seen on the carriage ride.

"Don't let yourself dream. He will distort the truth." He stopped abruptly, looking to the hall. "I'm sorry. I must go—I will be back for you."

And then, as quickly as he appeared, he was gone.

Before I could say anything, a short man in gaudy clothing and an oversized mask grabbed my arm and proceeded to twirl me around the room. I looked over the man's shoulder, trying to find my previous partner in the crowd, but he was nowhere to be found.

Edmund walked up to us, and the man came to an immediate halt. The man, who had tossed me around so carelessly, dropped his gaze as he shuffled off into a happy group of dancing couples. Edmund seemed to be satisfied. He quickly placed a hand around my shoulder and led me to a secluded area in the ballroom. We stood right beside a tall grandfather clock. I gave him my best fake smile and proceeded to watch him cautiously. The corners of his mouth turned slightly upward, indicating that he was pleased with my smile.

"You are stunning."

My face blushed immediately.

"I have something for you." His voice was soft and delicate. "Hold out your hands."

I held my hands out in front of me and curiously watched as he slid his hand into his frock—out came a sparkling egg. He gently placed the shimmering egg into my hands and then cupped his hands around mine. I looked down at our intertwined hands wrapped around the egg.

"What is it?" I asked anxiously.

"Patience, Clara. You will soon find out."

The clock began to chime. It was ten o'clock. My concentration was broken when I felt the egg shake between our hands. The egg was rocking—it was about to hatch. In a matter of moments, a small crack split down the center of the egg. I watched while a small white-and-brown head with two soft yellow eyes popped out of the opening. The egg wiggled in my hands again. The opening cracked again, so that the split was wide enough to observe the whole body of the chick. The small pile of feathers hopped out of the crumbling shell and perched on my wrist. Edmund slowly released his hands from mine to grab what was left of the empty shell. He placed the shell in his pocket before speaking.

"Look into his eyes," he said.

I held the soft bird to my cheek and then glanced into its yellow eyes. The eyes I had admired before became brighter and brighter until they were glowing an intense golden color.

"The great white owl is yours for life now." In a circular fashion, he waved his hand over the owl three times.

"Rector suus quod Servo suus, oh, *Valde Niveus!"* His voice sounded demanding.

I suddenly felt the weight of the hatchling increase. Surprised, I shot a glance to Edmund. He quickly and effortlessly grabbed my hands and tossed them into the air. The small owl hurled high into the air of the ballroom. I was frightened for the chick, knowing that any minute it would smash into the floor. But that didn't happen. Instead of the small owl falling to its death, it began to grow. I watched, fascinated—the chick transformed into a grand white owl. In seconds of crashing to the floor, the owl spread his wings and soared back to the high ceilings of the hall.

"Is this what magic feels like?"

"What do you feel?"

"My skin feels…tingly—almost like it's falling asleep."

"Yes, you are sensitive to the enchantment in the room." He stepped back, admiring the white owl. "Do you like your gift?"

"He's beautiful. Is everything here enchanted?"

"You ask too many questions." He chuckled.

"And you give few answers."

"There is not much for you to know. Only that I want you to be happy here and I will do whatever it takes to see that happen," he said. "Come—dance with me."

I found myself gliding across the ballroom floor again, back in his arms. Everyone danced all around us, laughing…smiling…kissing. The people seemed so carefree and happy. I wanted to be them.

The lighting of the great hall hushed to a twinkling glow as the music switched to a somber melody. I could sense the essence of a lullaby hidden in the dawdling harmony.

Edmund placed his hand on my neck and guided my head to his shoulder. I felt intoxicated by his touch. He looked at me once more with a crooked grin and slid his hand upward to remove my mask. In one fluid motion he had the mask off and falling to the ground. In my head the mask seemed to fall to the ground in slow motion—everything seemed to be moving in slow motion. I could no longer hear the obnoxious laughter of the crowd or the shuffling of feet, just the faint sound of a melodic violin playing underneath the sound of Edmund's humming.

"Are you happy?" He paused. "Are you happy here—with me?"

"I am, but there is one thing I long for." I lifted my head so that our eyes met. "Edmund—let me see you."

His grip on my hand tightened, while his body stiffened. "That is something I cannot allow."

"Why? What are you hiding? What are you not telling me?" I pleaded for answers, but they were hidden behind his tightened lips.

He was full of so many secrets, which surprisingly didn't bother me. But this one, I couldn't get past. A part of me felt like his face held some kind of truth I had been looking for—and he was keeping that truth from me. I wanted to know why. I swallowed loudly, trying to keep my emotions at bay.

Suddenly, a silence fell over the ballroom, and everything stopped. Those who had laughed loudly and danced around us carelessly only moments before were now hushed to a distinct silence, bowing toward the ballroom's newest arrival.

He was tall, much taller than Edmund, with an overall striking appearance. His eyes were the blackest of black, matching the long, silky hair that was combed back, folding slightly over his broad shoulders. I noticed his lips were sharply sculpted, as well as his dark eyebrows. His teeth and the white of his eyes shined as he smiled at the submission of the people bowing. The man dominated the room with his presence. It was hard not to watch him as he walked to the center platform and rested himself on the king's throne, Edmund's throne. With one gesture of his hand, he waved everyone off pause.

"Forget all of your questions. There is someone you are to meet."

Edmund looked down to my eyes, waiting until I met his gaze before escorting me to the throne. I'm not sure how he did it, but he had me in a haze again. Dazed. Confused. I would do anything he asked.

I followed him to the platform, until I stood facing the man of the hour.

"On high tides will the ocean bring—the nightingale who's lost her wings," the man said, standing from the throne. "So innocent, so beautiful you are." Each word rolled from his tongue with the most exotic tone.

Nightingale who's lost her wings. His words sounded familiar. I met the man's gaze, drawing a blank again. I wasn't sure what to make of him now that I was close. He appeared like a dark stallion, standing tall in my presence. *Who is he?* His fingers lightly touched the curve of his lips while he seemed to look me over.

"I am Victor," he said.

I nodded, too intimidated to respond.

His hand reached out to graze my face; I flinched from the startling cold. There was something remarkably similar about him and Edmund, something distant and sinister, but undeniably beautiful and alluring.

A loud crackling sounded from overhead, distracting me from his touch. My eyes automatically glanced up to see the owl flying toward the throne. The sound was coming from the regal creature. The moment the owl touched the back of the throne, there was another loud crackling sound, followed by a hiss, and then silence. The owl had frozen into stone before my eyes.

I glared at Victor, assuming he was to blame. "What did you do to him?"

While Victor laughed at my concern, Edmund stepped in front of me to calm me down. "There's no need to be upset. He is yours, and you are his. Your touch will awaken him."

My eyes flickered up through my eyelashes at Edmund. "Why did he turn him to stone?"

"He did not turn your owl to stone." He continued, "The owl will turn to stone when it is time for him to rest." He explained with such a calm voice, that I believed him without another question.

"Come," he instructed while guiding me down the platform. "I think you should retire for the evening." He smiled. "May I see you once more before the night is over?"

"I thought you said I should go to my room."

"Yes, you see, I have another surprise for you, but I would like to share it in private."

"Another surprise?"

"Will you consent to the midnight rendezvous, then?"

"I will consent." I twirled my dress and then squeezed his gloved hands. "But only if we can meet in the library."

With his nod of approval, I gave an enthusiastic smile and then made my way to the spiral staircase. I could feel his stare watch my every step up the stairs, until I was completely out of sight.

Once I made my way through the two golden doors to the hallway, I closed them behind me and leaned back against their cold surface. I rested there, thinking about the night—about Edmund. I decided not to worry about Victor or the stranger and his warning—not now when everything seemed perfect. I finally pushed myself from the doors and twirled down the hall, humming the melody of the dark waltz. I was finally happy.

As I danced past the portraits and sword displays in the hall, I came to the hall ending with the red door. Edmund was persistent that I never enter the room, but I had a strange desire to take a peek. I looked down the hall; there was no one behind or in front of me. I walked quickly and quietly to the door and slowly turned the knob. With one fast tug to the door, I realized the room was locked. I stood there for a moment, thinking about leaving and going to my room. But my curiosity got the best of me.

I pulled the pearl hairpin from my hair and gently slipped it into the keyhole of the door. It was a long shot, but worth a try. I twisted the pin again and again, wiggling the door handle, until I finally heard a click. *Bull's-eye.* I was in.

I caught a chill the moment I stepped into the room. The chill reminded me that I was not welcome and that I should turn back, but my curiosity encouraged me to look around. I stood there with my body glued to the back of the door until my eyes adjusted to my new surroundings. After a few moments, I noticed a small beam of moonlight shining through a floor-length window nestled in the left corner of the room. I automatically walked toward the light.

With one step I saw books and other hidden objects scattered across the floor. I shuffled my feet through books and rubble until I was standing in the light from the window. The light beams reflected off a golden mantel. Hanging crooked above its dusty surface was an aged painting. I brushed my fingers over the canvas.

Underneath the mask of dirt was a portrait of a family. At my first glance, I simply saw a proud mother and father sitting in tall chairs with two happy boys leaning against them. But when I dusted the painting a little more, I noticed that the mother and father were sitting in royal chairs and were wearing crowns.

The minutes passed slowly as I studied the painting. It was fascinating; every piece of the canvas was painted in great detail. The mother wore a lovely silk dress that fit tightly around her small waist and then puffed out like a bell around her. The father sat tall in dark blue attire, with the fabric from his shoulders sculpted like small pillows. The boys matched their father in similar clothing. What caught my attention was a small sparkling pendant that hung from their necks and rested on the blue fabric of their vests. I was unable to make out the design of the pendant, but I thought it was interesting that they both had one. I imagined the family in the portrait lived a glamorous life, filled with masquerades and fancy dinners. And I couldn't help but wonder if this was Edmund's family.

I quietly began to maneuver my way through the books to the window. The floor-length window opened to an outside balcony that overlooked the crashing waves of the ocean. I pressed my face to the cool glass to get a better view. The bold moon reflected off the waves from beneath and seemed to bounce upward to the balcony and into the room.

I suddenly felt a tingle in my legs, like the magic I had felt before. It was time for me to leave. I frantically turned around to make my way back through my path and to the door. In my frenzy I miscalculated a step, tripped, and fell straight into a mound of broken wood and pages of ripped books. Surprisingly, I did not create much noise from my fall, but I lay terrified that someone might have heard.

When I lifted myself from the floor, I noticed that my palm had landed on a ripped portrait. I carefully flipped the torn flaps of canvas back into place until a partial face of an older boy came into focus. Even with missing pieces, the face was breathtaking. I traced the outline of his broad chin to his beautiful smile and then up to the perfect lines of his nose, until stopping on the tear where his eyes should have been. Something about the painting moved me. I wanted to know who he was. My hands slid over the bottom of the painting, where another piece of the torn canvas hung loosely. I gasped as I moved the piece back into place.

There, around his neck, rested the same pendant that lay against my skin. I hurriedly pulled the necklace off and held the cross medallion against the painting. There was no mistake—it was the same. Immediately, I fastened the necklace back around my neck and then threw my hands into the mound of debris surrounding the painting. I had to find the missing piece.

I shifted books and lifted broken pieces of furniture for several minutes. I didn't see anything that resembled the missing piece of canvas. I looked at the doorway and back down, frustrated. The small tingle of magic that I had felt before was growing stronger. I told myself that I would only search for a few more minutes, and then I would have to leave. I leaned forward, pushed the bottom of my dress behind me, and then scrambled on my hands and knees until I reached another mound of rubble. Only seconds into this pile, I found exactly what I was looking for—the last piece of the puzzle. Anxiously, I crawled back to the painting and lightly slid the last piece into place.

His eyes were emerald with flakes of luminous gold and amber swirled around the edges. I could have sat there daydreaming about the boy in the picture for the rest of the night, but my cautious instinct told me otherwise. I carefully folded the last piece of the canvas and tucked it into the top of my dress, next to the pendant. The prickling sensation was becoming hard to ignore. I didn't understand how magic worked, but anytime I was near Edmund or anything that was unearthly beautiful, I could feel it—like a chill that engulfed my whole body.

From outside the door, I heard the familiar clicking of Edmund's boots against the tile of the hallway. The clicking stopped, and I knew he was standing on the other side of the red door. I stood frozen with terror.

Just before the door cracked opened, I felt a warm hand run across my mouth and a quick tug on my waist. My body was instantly enveloped in a warm embrace. The strong arms pulled me backward, faster than my mind could comprehend. The wall behind us appeared to open and swallow us up.

I tried to control my breathing, but my heart was racing from the surprise. I didn't know if I should thank the person who held me tight or fight to escape. I squirmed out of response.

"Stay still," a voice whispered in my ear.

I felt the strong tingle of magic now; I knew Edmund was in the room. I heard another set of footsteps enter and immediately pushed further back into the stranger's arms.

"Everything is going as planned. The girl doesn't know what to believe. She will be yours in two days' time." It was Victor.

"There must be another way."

"We had an agreement. If you wish to end your hunger for this ridiculous love—if you wish for her to be your queen—you will honor it!"

"Those are my wishes," Edmund replied. "But I do not want her to suffer as I have suffered."

I heard Victor's boots kicking through the debris on the floor. "You call this suffering?" Victor's voice was filled with a growing rage. "I have given you power. I have given you a kingdom! You will live an eternal life of beauty!"

"All for what? I eat, but do not taste. I touch, but do not feel. I love, but will never be loved. I can't bear to look at my own reflection! You took it all from me and replaced it with nothing. That is my suffering!"

"You will have your love as soon as she's crowned queen. She will be yours throughout eternity."

"She is not meant to be a dark angel. This is my curse, not hers."

"Listen to me! You will do as I command. Turn her tonight before the clock strikes midnight, or I will take her soul myself!"

There was a moment of silence, and then I heard Edmund's voice softly mutter, "It will be done."

I cringed in the darkness as my mind processed what I had heard. I was experiencing one nightmare after the next. Behind me the stranger began to inch backward, pulling me with him. We slowly and quietly stepped further away from the room, until I realized we were in another secret tunnel.

"It's time to go," he said anxiously. This time I recognized his voice. It was the same voice from the stranger who had warned me about Edmund.

"You were at the ball," I said below my breath. "Who are you?"

"My name is Finn. I'm here to help you," he said. "Now we must hurry—we need to get outside these walls before he realizes you are missing."

His fingers wrapped around my wrist, and he began to tug. The stranger had been right about Edmund. I had no choice but to follow him now. I blinked my eyes hard in the darkness, trying to make out the turns, but there was not enough light. He whipped us through the tunnels as if he had them memorized.

He finally stopped when we turned down a tunnel that ended in square stones. I watched as he forced one of the stones loose, and then another, creating an opening just large enough to crawl through. I felt a breeze push through the opening, carrying a salty smell.

"Keep your head down when you surface," he muttered.

Outside, darkness had settled in. I knelt to the ground as soon as I pulled my legs from the stone hole and surveyed the surroundings. To my left was rocky land, dropping down into the dark ocean water. To my right was the very place where Edmund had taken me the day before. The passage had led us just outside the castle walls.

"Where are we going? There's nothing out here," I questioned as soon as he surfaced.

"To the forest. Take off your shoes," he said. "We run from here."

We ran straight for the trees, and I felt every sharp rock along the way.

This forest was not as inviting as the forest of pine light. The moon was hidden, the trees were dark, not a single twinkle of light. I heard wolves crying and saw owls scattering in the trees, but the man I followed didn't seem to mind. He ran with purpose.

As soon as the castle was out of sight, I stopped to catch my breath. "Are you going to tell me what's going on?"

"I would think it would be quite obvious by now."

"Well, it's not," I growled, but he seemed to be focused on our surroundings.

"We need to keep moving. It's not far from here," he said. "Just stay with me."

Stay with me. His words reminded me of my dream.

We finally came to the end of the forest, where the land dropped into the ocean. A sticky fog hid the water, but you could still hear it rippling below. Finn leaned over the edge, looking through the cloud, and then let out a low whistle.

Suddenly, a wooden angel appeared out of the fog. His wings were swept back in the air, while his arm held a sword stretched over the ocean water. As the angel neared, I could see the ship to which he belonged. There were no patches in the ship's sails or holes in its hull. The wood had a dark cherry finish, instead of the rough and faded wood of the ship that had once been my prison. The sails were taller; the body was longer, sleeker. It floated fearlessly in the water, much like the angel.

"Hold your breath."

"Wh—?" Before I finished the word, his arms were locked around me and we were falling down into the ocean.

I was furious when I surfaced from the water.

"Are...you...crazy?" I asked as I spit the remaining ocean out of my mouth.

"We had to get to the ship," he said. I could have sworn he was smirking when he started to swim away. "Come on."

The closer we were to the hull of the ship, the more magnificent it seemed. Ropes quickly dropped over the sides, lifting us from the water to its deck.

It took my eyes a moment to scan over the faces of the men on board, but then I saw a familiar face pushing through the crowd. *My beloved Fergus.* I had so much to say to him, so much to apologize for, but he got to me so quickly and held me so tightly that I didn't have a chance to say a thing.

"I know, Clara. I know," he said as if he could read my thoughts. "Let's get you into something dry."

As he helped me to the captain's quarters, I turned to take one more curious look back. There was a lot of commotion, men laughing and congratulating Finn for his victory, but his eyes were on me. *There's something about him.* I nervously darted my eyes back to Fergus and stepped into the cabin.

I was able to apologize to Fergus as he bandaged my sore feet. I told him I was sorry for not believing him and that I was even more sorry for getting upset at him.

"You had every right to be upset," he said. "It's in the past now."

As we talked, everything started rushing back. *Erik. Alice. The chase.* While I had been at the castle, something had clouded my memory; something had pushed them out of my thoughts.

"Alice," I said. "She's here, isn't she?"

Fergus slowly raised himself from my bandaged feet and sat next to me on the bed. "Yes, this is where they brought her."

"Why? What is this world? How are we connected?"

"This world has been here since the beginning of time. It's the place of good and evil—of light and darkness. And it's connected to the world you know in every way." He paused. "Alice was brought here to ensure you would return."

"Who are these people that are after us?"

"The fallen ones."

My mind raced to Maytide and her warning about the fallen angels. *The dark ones. The vampyres. The process.* She had tried to tell me all along.

"Is Erik one of them?"

"I'm afraid so. He once was a great guardian, before he fell from grace—before he was marked. We didn't know he had fallen until he came after you."

"A guardian?"

"Yes. Just like you and I, he was a defender for all that is good. A protector of the gateway between worlds."

"I don't understand."

"There are a select few who are chosen to be guardians. And even less that are born with a special gift. It's in their blood. It's their destiny. You are one, just like your father. You are chosen to protect this land from evil and to keep that evil from leaving this place."

I'm a guardian? How was that possible? I couldn't protect myself, much less anyone else.

"What do you mean I was born with a special gift? What kind of gift?"

"Every guardian is different, and every gift develops in its own time. Yours will come when the time is right. Your father was blessed with the gift of strength when he was only a boy. He was incredibly strong. It made him almost indestructible in battle."

"Almost?"

"Well, we still don't know." I could tell that Fergus still struggled with the idea that my father was gone.

"What's your gift?" I questioned, trying to ease his mind from the pain.

"Your father was my gift." He smiled. "And storytelling."

I leaned to Fergus, placing my head on his shoulder and my hand on top of his. I was glad he was here. I was glad that he was my grandfather. I only hoped he knew this. Fergus gently squeezed my hand and then carefully stood from the bed.

"I believe we both need to rest," he said. "We will talk more tomorrow. Good night, my sweet grandchild."

"Good night."

-20-

FINAL STORY

I SLEPT AN ENTIRE DAY BEFORE WAKING TO THE SOUND OF an overactive accordion. I sat up in the bed and looked to the small golden windows that lined the side of the cabin. There was no daylight shining through. *What time is it?*

Suddenly, there was a light tap on the door.

"Sorry to barge in," Fergus said, smiling apologetically. "I thought you should know we are about to serve dinner on deck."

"Dinner?" I was surprised to find that I had slept through breakfast and lunch.

"Yes, and it's a beautiful night for dancing," he continued. "There's fresh clothes for you in the cabinet. Finn made sure of that."

I flashed another smile. "Fergus?"

"Yes, dear."

"Could you tell me where we are?"

"We are only three days' journey to the plummet." His face was abruptly serious.

"The plummet?"

"The Devil's Backbone. The entrance to the land of Hades. That's where they take all the prisoners. That's where Alice will be."

"Why is it called the plummet?"

"Don't worry about these things, child. I'll get her back," he said. "Now—get dressed and join us on deck." With a half-hearted smile, Fergus slipped through the cabin door, into the loud music.

After changing into a simple pale blue dress, I noticed a bowl of fresh water next to the wardrobe. I used this to clean my face and hands before stepping out into the crisp, clean air.

The men were all scattered around the deck, some eating, some dancing; all were singing to the tunes of the accordion. I caught several men glancing and smiling as I walked passed them to Finn. He stood alone at the front of the ship, staring out into the starry night sky.

"Finn?" He turned, and for the first time, I saw his face. I openly stared for a moment, gawking at his undeniable beauty.

"It was you—you are the boy from the painting."

"That was a long time ago." His eyes darted back to the sea.

"You are the son of a king."

"And you are the daughter of a guardian."

It was strange at first to be that close without staring into a mask. I felt like I was looking right into the painting again—marveling at an undeniable splendor.

"You knew me before, didn't you?"

Finn's eyes narrowed—I could tell he was in deep thought. We stood there, leaning against the wood of the ship for several silent minutes.

"My father was king of Everest," he said, breaking the silence. "And your father was the greatest of all guardians—my father's most trusted knight. You and your mother would stay in the castle when the guardians left for war. Our families became very close. As children we would play in the woods, skipping stones across the stream."

I stared at his profile, trying to imagine every word he spoke. I could almost see a stream in my mind, but it vanished as quickly as the next wave swept under the ship. I looked back to his picturesque face. It was in a subtle change of expression that I noticed his sadness. I watched as his eyes slowly curved down and his soft smile transformed into a bitter frown. I could tell that it was hard for him to look back into his own memories.

"In one night everything changed," he said, keeping his eyes focused on the sea.

"What happened that night? I need to know."

"I failed to keep you safe—I failed to save my family and to protect yours." His voice was bleak. "I should have died that night. I didn't deserve to live."

I saw his fist clench at his side while he looked into the distance.

"Who did this?"

"He that bears the mark of the damned."

"I want a name," I demanded, feeling that I had every right to know who had ripped my family apart.

"It was at the end of Victor's blade my family fell and his schemes that tore yours apart." I could hear the fury in his voice, but he kept it tight and under control. "Edmund was his pawn. He gave Victor all that he needed to penetrate our defense and to destroy our kingdom. I swore to take my revenge on them both."

Edmund. Victor. I felt a spasm of rage in my chest, recognizing I had been face-to-face with the ones who had ruined my life, and had done nothing. Edmund's scent still remained in my hair. Victor's face still burned in my mind. I stepped carefully over the piles of rope that blanketed the deck, to lean against the dark wood that made up the side of the ship. Through the wind and mists of salt water, I could feel Finn staring, silently waiting for a response.

The silence was abruptly interrupted when a shipmate poked his head from the stairs of the lower deck and yelled excitedly across the ship. "Captain…Aye, Captain! We need to speak with ye…"

Another crew member popped up beside the man and with a chuckle said, "Come on, Cap'in Finn…Don't make good men wait!"

Finn shook his head and apologized for their abruptness. "Are you all right?"

"I will be."

"Let me check on them. Last time I made them wait, they caught the ship on fire."

I politely nodded, then watched as he trotted across the deck and made his way down the stairway. He passed Fergus as he disappeared from my line of sight.

"They will pay for what they have done, child," Fergus said as he limped over to my side.

"But why did they do this to us?"

"With the royal family dead, the guardians are the only defense against Victor's power. If we are gone, then the resistance will fail, and there will be no one left to protect this world from his evil schemes.

Victor would have complete power over this land. Nothing would stop him from entering the gateways," he said.

"And why Edmund? Why is he a part of this?"

"He was tempted, just like the rest. Only he had a gift that Victor saw fit for a king," Fergus said grimly. "Edmund was a guardian, gifted with the power to change one's perceptions. Victor wanted Edmund as the king of Everest, to be the dark angel that would lead this kingdom into his darkness."

I thought back to the castle and the meadow. The times I had witnessed his perfect mirage waver.

"Why? Why would he do this?"

"For love, Clara. He was promised you as his queen," he said. "It is said that he was besieged with such guilt, that his own reflection haunted him. So he concealed his face with a mask."

I gripped the side of the ship, digging my nails into the wood. How could I have been so naive? I thought of how close I had been to him, how attracted I had been, how trusting I was. I thought of how frightening it was to hear him speak to Victor, to hear that I was promised to him, that I belonged to him, and for him to say, *"It will be done."* When I was finally able to speak, I wanted to know more about my family. I wanted to know why Victor wanted my soul.

"What happened to my family, Fergus? Did Edmund kill them? Are we all that is left?"

"I don't know what happened to your mother and father." He paused to blink back tears. "Your father had been away at war the night of the attack.

And your mother, she was staying in the castle with you. I'm afraid you were the last one to see them both."

I felt my face turn hot and my eyes burn, trying to hold back raw emotion.

"There are not many guardians left, Clara. Most were killed or turned to the dark ways. Those are the ones who lead the fallen through the gateways."

"Like Erik?"

"Yes, like Erik."

"Why did they come after me?"

"There is only one female guardian born every five hundred years. And that guardian is gifted with a powerful gift, the only gift that can destroy Victor. You are that guardian," he said. "Victor wants your soul; he wants that power. That is why we have kept you hidden these past years. We were waiting for you to remember. We were waiting for your gift to develop."

"If it was my soul he wanted, why did he not take it that night?"

"Victor cannot take a soul. It must be given to him freely. He tried to tempt you, like the others, but your faith was too strong," he said. "So he took the only thing he could."

I knew immediately what had been stolen from me, but Fergus confirmed it all the same.

"Your memories," he said. "He stole your memories."

I stood there for a few quiet minutes, still focusing on the swells of the ocean, taking in all that I had heard.

“This was the final story I had to tell you.” He gently slipped a bound leather journal into my hand. “I believe this belongs to you. It will help you find your way.”

I looked down to see the leather book, a book I thought I had lost for good. Here I was struggling again, trying to hold back my emotions. I looked back up to him and felt the tears fall.

-21-

MONSTER

ON THE THIRD DAY OF OUR JOURNEY, THE SKIES BLACKENED and the sea released a fury that no one expected. All afternoon the crew slid across the deck, pulling and tugging at ropes, fighting against the ocean to keep us afloat.

Then an odd thing happened—the roaring of the waves ceased, and the ocean became smooth as glass. All of the men lined the sides of the ship, looking over at the water's smooth surface. Before I had time to walk over to examine the water, there was a loud crack and a jolt from underneath the ship. The men continued to look over the side, staring into the water. I heard them talking among one another.

"Did we hit land?" a tall man shouted.

The man beside him responded, "That's impossible."

"Maybe a whale," I heard another man suggest.

We had not hit land, nor had a whale bumped against the hull of the ship. I looked down and caught a brief glimpse of something in the water. It was definitely not a whale.

A long, rigid backbone sliced through the ocean and circled the ship, taunting us like prey. The body of the creature was similar to that of an alligator, but gray and the size of a bus. The body propelled itself several yards out of the water, revealing the fierce identity of the sea creature. I had never seen anything like it. Its head was short and flat—its snout long. It nipped at the ship with razor-sharp teeth the size of daggers. Its body was built to shoot itself out of the water using two long, bony fins. And it was covered in black and gray scales—thousands of them.

It shot out of the water again. This time it was much higher, latching on to one of the decorative rails and snapping it off like a twig. It fell back to the water with the rail still crunching between its jaws.

There was a bump from the back of the ship and then from the front. A hit on the left side of the ship and then the right. A short, rounded man, one who had stared at me on more than one occasion, leaned over the rail to get a better look. Before anyone could advise him otherwise, the massive creature shot out of the water and grabbed the man. It wasn't much of a struggle. The creature took him down into the ocean before he had time to fight back.

I almost threw up. Blood had pooled on the deck where the man had last been standing. That was all that was left of him, just blood. Finn pushed me further back to the captain's quarters and ordered me to go inside. As much as I wanted to hide from everything, I couldn't hide while he and Fergus were left exposed to the danger on deck. I just couldn't do it.

Everyone pushed to the center of the ship, blades drawn and eyes glued to their surroundings. Any minute the reptile could fly into the sky and grab any one of them. But it didn't. It was waiting. Waiting for someone to get too close.

Fergus yelled out to everyone, “Help me move the cockboat—I have an idea!”

I watched as the men carefully unfastened one of the cockboats from the front of the deck. Fergus climbed inside.

“You,” Fergus said, pointing to a young man, “climb to the crow’s nest and signal when and where you see the creature. Signal when he moves.” The man took off and, as instructed, began his climb to the crow’s nest. Fergus looked to the men who had crowded around him. “Lower me down to the water in the boat. I will gut the creature when it jumps from the water—when its belly is exposed.”

No one seemed to question him. I caught a reassuring look from his eyes as they scooted the small boat to the edge of the ship, to the same spot that was filled with pools of a dead man’s blood. Finn was right there amongst the men—his muscles tight from the weight of the boat, his brow gleaming with sweat. The man on lookout gave a signal as soon as they reached the edge. Fergus nodded to Finn, and they steadily began to lower him down the hull of the ship.

No one wanted to look over the edge to see what happened, but I ran to the side as soon as I heard the man in the crow’s nest yell, “Look out!”

The reptile sprang from the water, its jaw open, its tail flapping through the air; it flew right over the small boat. Fergus plunged his sword into the soft underbelly of the creature, and its own body weight ripped it open. It landed on the cockboat, pulling the ropes from the side of the ship. I watched as Fergus, the boat, and the snapping monster fell into the quiet, dark waters.

"Fergus!" I cried. "Someone do something!"

No one knew if Fergus or the creature were still alive. The same man who had cried out the warning shouted from above, "I can't see Fergus! I can't see the creature!"

And just as he shouted, there was another splash overboard. *Finn.*

I leaned further over the edge, trying to see through the water. It was too dark to see anything. "Please, God. Please, please, God. Let them be all right," I said to myself. Now that I had them both back in my life, I couldn't lose them again. They surfaced to the water simultaneously, gasping for the night air. Finn had an arm looped around Fergus, keeping him afloat. Fergus was bleeding. A device was quickly lowered to them, and they were hoisted back to the safety of the ship.

The creature was dead, but it had managed to nip Fergus during the fall into the ocean. His hand was pressed to the oozing wound when I got to him. It was a nasty gash, but thanks to Finn's rescue, he would survive. We helped him to the captain's quarters, where I cleaned and dressed the wound as best as I knew how. It was a deep cut, but it hadn't punctured any organs. I thanked God for that.

"What were you thinking? You could have been killed," I said through tear-filled eyes.

"Oh, Clara—it is more important to see that you are kept safe." Fergus raised a hand to swipe away a single tear that had rolled down to my chin. "You needn't worry about me. I'll be all right."

"You don't understand—I can't lose you again." I looked to Finn. "I can't lose either one of you again."

Fergus took my hands in his and lightly kissed them both. "I understand," he whispered. Finn's eyes never left mine.

But they didn't understand. I loved them. That's what I wanted to say. That's what I was trying to say—but I just didn't know how. I fell asleep sitting on the floor with my head against the bed and my hands still in his. Finn never left the room either.

There were no more monsters that night. Only heroes.

-22-

THE DEVIL'S BACKBONE

AT DAWN WE SAW IT—AN ISLAND APPEARED FROM THE SEA. A raging pile of jungle would be a better description. Twisted palms were waving high in the sky from the very breeze that had carried us over the sea. From a distance, the island looked like a tropical paradise—but as we neared, you could see this was no paradise.

I dressed in men's clothes that morning. It was either that or a dress. The tan faded pants fit pretty good considering, and so did the white long-sleeve shirt—after I tucked it in the pants and ripped off the long sleeves. I found a leather side pouch, which surprisingly was similar to the bags I carried to school. I decided to take the book of poems with me.

There was a knock on the door. Fergus entered with a bulging napkin, which I quickly found to be food for the journey.

"Sea biscuits," he said. "They taste like crackers from back home." He hobbled over to the bed and sat down to pack the food into my bag. "There should be plenty of bacon and salted meat to give you energy. The salted meat doesn't look pretty, but you will find that it tastes like jerky. The men have already filled a boat with plenty of fresh water for you both. It is very important that you have eaten and that you are fully hydrated before you fall into Hades."

Fall. What a nightmare—a nightmare I would be living sooner than I'd hoped. I plopped down on the bed next to Fergus and leaned to him, like a scared child would to her father. The day was finally here. All these years I had been looking for someone to blame—someone to hate. Soon I would be standing on the precipice, peering down into a dark place that held the answers to my stolen past. Literally. I would find my truth. I would find the person who was to blame. And if I survived the fall, I would see my aunt again.

Fergus placed a hand on each of my shoulders. "I'm sorry I cannot make this journey with you," he said. His injury from the night before had left him temporarily crippled on one side—unable to lift a weapon. It was hard for him to accept that he had to stay on the ship. Fergus had always watched over me—always protected me, even when I was unaware I needed protecting. He was there. This time he couldn't be, and his devastation was enough to touch the coldest of hearts. His warm gaze lingered for a moment. I felt security pass from his eyes to mine. It was time to go.

I stood and aided Fergus in raising his own weight from the bed. I've never seen him so sad—so vulnerable. In my eyes, even though he was pushing seventy, Fergus embodied strength and hope. Those personifications were decaying right before my eyes—fading piece by piece from his devastation. I could hardly bear to see it.

Finn entered the cabin. "It's time, Clara," he said.

I nodded in response. I was ready—ready as I could be, given I didn't know what to expect. This was my time to be brave, my time to step up. Too long had I relied on the strength of others; too long had I run from my fears.

Fergus darted his eyes to Finn as he hugged me one last time. "Please, bring her back to me."

"You have my word," Finn said.

The crew had already readied the cockboat over the side of the ship. Finn stepped into the swinging boat and held my hand as I did the same. As we were lowered down the side of the hull, Fergus leaned over with one last piece of advice.

"Remember to use your faith to stand against the evil one and his schemes. He is not of flesh and blood—he cannot be defeated as if he was. Everything in Hades will be against you. The elements will be severe. The entire land will be a manifestation of your fears. Do not give in to those fears—it will give him control," he yelled.

The boat dropped to the water with a bounce, spraying us both with a salty mist. The paddles split through the ocean water and guided the tip of the boat away from the ship, away from safety. We didn't speak. It seemed easier that way.

The air on the island was heavy with moisture—at times the air was so thick that you could taste the elements of the jungle on your tongue. There were hundreds of different trees mingled together—so many that they actually formed a canopy over our heads. Only small beams of light were able to penetrate through the tiny cracks in the awning. Animals and insects chirped and bellowed and squawked. Monkeys scrambled from branch to branch. Mosquitoes and flies circled our heads. We trudged through it all.

Finn led the way, of course, knocking down limbs, carefully helping me over fallen trees. He would stop periodically to listen to the jungle and to point out poisonous plants.

"Manchineel tree," he said. "Don't go near it."

Its bark was gray, like many of the trees we had seen, but its branches were covered with perfectly shaped green leaves, bright yellow flowers, and lush apple-like fruit. It was enticing. The apples looked so tasty. *If only I had one bite.* My mouth watered.

"But—its fruit looks ripe. It's just an apple." I was mesmerized by it.

"Not from that tree—don't take anything from that tree. The manchineel is the most poisonous tree in this world and in your world. One bite of its fruit is fatal. One slight bump against its bark will cause your skin to buckle and blister. Even when burned, its smoke will cause blindness. The very sap it leaks is used on the arrows of our enemies. Victor is known for using these trees to torture our people. Ripping their clothes from their body—tying them to its trunk. All you can do is scream while your skin bubbles from your body."

Even the trees are against us, I thought. My face must have twisted to show what I was thinking, because he turned back around to clear a new path. We continued to travel deep into the island, twisting in and out of trees and dodging brightly colored flowers.

The day disappeared quickly in the jungle. Night swept in under the canopy of trees, trapping the dark around us. I was nervous about stopping. Stopping meant that Finn and I would be in one place at the same time, with nothing or no one to distract us from having a real conversation.

He stopped and listened to the night. *What is he listening for?* I wished I knew. Whatever he heard or didn't hear seemed to please him. He threw his leather satchel to the ground. I did the same with mine. I guessed this was camp.

He leaned down and grabbed two small items from his bag. From what I could see, he was holding a red rock, speckled with black spots, and a piece of metal.

"What's that?"

"Jasper and iron. We need to have a fire going before it gets much darker. Grab a few of those leaves." He pointed with his head to an area underneath a tree that was covered in tangled roots. "Only the dead leaves," he said.

Finn stepped over to a thin tree and broke off several branches. He strategically placed those in a pile in the clearing. He then pulled out a small dagger and moved to a different tree, a tree stamped with fungus of different shapes, colors, and sizes. With his dagger he cut two pieces of fungus from the tree. I noticed they were the same—white, gray striped, and rounded, like the hooves of a horse. He scraped the fungus with his dagger and then sat the exposed layer on the ground. I had read about this once. It was some article I ran across at the library—"Surviving in the Wild," it was called. Never in a million years would I have expected this to be practical information. If I recalled correctly, he was about to use the fungus as tinder—as a substance to ignite the fire.

Sparks flew. I had recalled correctly. He leaned down and blew softly, gently. I stared at his lips. He fed the spark a few dry leaves and then small twigs. In minutes, we had a fire.

We both unpacked our bags. He poured water into two wooden cups. I handed him a biscuit while I crunched on mine. We sat near the fire against the trunk of a fallen tree. I finished one biscuit and gulped down the full cup of water Finn had poured for me. It was sweet with a mango flavor—it was refreshing. I was getting more nervous.

"More water?" he asked.

"Please."

His hand slid over mine when he reached for my cup. It was warm and electric. He pulled away and seemed to shudder, as if he was repelled by the swift connection our bodies had made.

"Thanks," I said. I took another sip. I felt awkward.

"We will reach the summit by noon tomorrow," he announced sharply.

I sighed, disappointed that our conversation was going nowhere.

"Is something wrong?" He looked cautious.

"Yes," I blurted. "Something is wrong. You are keeping something from me." I scooted my back closer to the trunk of the tree so that I was sitting up tall. "We are going through hell itself tomorrow—so, I think I deserve to know why you keep pushing me away."

He was silent.

"Look at me," I said softly as I waited for his attention. "Look," I repeated. His gaze finally met mine. I could see the flame reflecting in his eyes. They seemed so dark, so unexpectedly dark. But then they softened into the electric green I had seen in the eyes of his portrait, with a warm ring of gold around them.

"It's hard to be close to you," he said.

"Oh." I hadn't expected that response.

"All these years," he muttered, "I thought you were dead."

His sad eyes pierced right through me, causing me to hold my breath. We both looked away, breaking the gaze simultaneously, struck by the same hesitant feeling.

"Now that you are here, alive, you have made me weak. Because now—I have something to lose. This thought consumes me with every breath. If I lose you again, there will be nothing left of me, only an empty shell of a man." He paused, pushing his hair from his face. "So don't be offended if I keep my distance. You are still something I recover from."

I stared ahead, catching glimpses of his chest rising and falling in the dimming light of the fire. I was taking shallow breaths now, nervous from my own thoughts. I knew that he was important to me; I could feel something stir deep in my heart, in my soul. And he appeared to feel something, too—but what was this electric tension between us?

I patiently waited, hoping that he had more to say—but anxious about what it might be. After a few minutes of waiting and sporadic breathing, he turned his body so that he faced me. His hand lightly touched the side of my neck, tracing the lines down to the pendant hidden under my blouse.

"I gave this to you the last time I saw you." He smiled as the pine light from the cross began to glow. "It was very dear to me. I'm glad you kept it safe."

"Would you like it back?" I asked, not knowing what else to say.

"No, it is yours. I like seeing it around your neck."

His bright green eyes scanned over the pendant one more time before he placed it back against my skin.

We ate the rest of our dinner, staring quietly at the fire. Finn got up a few times to stir the logs, but eventually settled back down beside me. Before long, the warmth of the fire had wrapped me like a blanket, bringing sleep with it. The urge to close my eyes took precedence over staying awake. I slowly fell into my first dreamless sleep.

-23-

PLUMMET

THE NEXT THING I KNEW, IT WAS DAWN, AND MY HEAD WAS on Finn's chest. His arm was underneath my neck, resting on my shoulder in a protective embrace. I'm not sure how it got there; I just knew that I liked it being there. I looked up, secretly admiring the exquisiteness of his face, wondering how I could have ever forgotten such a face.

After waking, we quickly filled our stomachs with the remaining sea biscuits, salted meat, and bacon. We doused the fire and began our meander through the jungle once more. I wasn't paying as much attention to the trees this time; my eyes were occupied studying Finn. I noted how he wrinkled his brow when I spoke to him, how he pushed his thick hair from his face when we stopped for water, how he wiped the sweat from his forehead when the humidity was almost unbearable. Before long his shirt was halfway open, giving me even more to study.

His skin was darker than I had noticed before, almost golden, like a Brazilian tan. And he was buff—boy, was he buff. Now that I looked, I could see the ripples of muscles in his chest and the tight lines of his back. Then a surprise breeze caught the fabric of his shirt, revealing something else. A scar. It was slightly to the left of his heart, noticeably lighter in color, a few inches long and half an inch wide.

I wanted to ask him about it, but was unsure how to bring it up. Then Finn stopped dead in his tracks and I didn't have to—I had something else to wonder about.

I pushed through the branches that separated us, until I could see what had frozen him.

There was a small clearing, with a pool of water, situated between two dead trees. The pool was oddly sized, only a few yards long and wide. And the water was dark blue, not what I expected from a pool of still water. No grass grew in the clearing. No jungle bush or flower. And there were no animals in the trees around it. Finn grabbed my arm when I attempted to step past him for a better look.

"This is it," he said. "The plummet."

"This? This is the plummet?" It seemed an odd place for something so foreboding.

"Yes. This is where we fall."

Now I understood.

Finn eased his way to the edge of the water, instructing me to stay behind him. I was tense with every step we made.

"We jump together," he said, reaching for my hand. "Are you ready?"

Was I ready to jump into a dark pool of uncertainty? Was I ready to fall into hell itself? An honest answer wouldn't have made a good answer, so I nodded as convincingly as I could. Finn gave me one last look, and then we jumped.

Faceless bodies pulled us down into the deep water. They were everywhere—floating and swirling around us while we struggled to hold our breath. I had never seen anything so demonic. Finn wrapped his arms around my waist and hugged my body as we were pulled down into the abyss. The water was ice-cold and clear as we descended. I looked over his shoulder to see the bodies scatter as we dropped into darker water.

It looked like we were dropping into a giant crack in the floor of the ocean. As we neared the fracture, I could see hundreds of tube-like clusters lining the floor of the ocean like carpet. Each tube resembled a different size worm—some were small; others were long enough to wrap around our bodies. I couldn't help but tighten my grip around Finn's chest while we lowered through the colony of worm creatures into the abyss.

Once we entered the darkness, I closed my eyes and clung to Finn's neck. I was afraid of what might happen next.

Suddenly, the temperature of the water began to drop. I opened my eyes to see a blurry red surface of water growing closer. I loosened my grip around Finn so that we could kick at the water beneath us. In seconds we popped from an icy lake, where we took our first gasp of air in Hades.

-24-

HADES

THE SKY WAS BLACK, NO MOON OR STAR IN SIGHT. THE ONLY light came from a ruby glow surrounding a distant mountain. The stench of smoke filled our lungs as we crawled from the icy water to the bank and rolled into the snow. My bones ached from the kicking and the fast drop in temperature. I had never felt this kind of cold. The combination of water with the icy atmosphere made it difficult to breathe. Both our bodies were shaking.

For the first time, the danger felt real. We were both wet to the bone and surrounded by the feeling of death. I was afraid. Finn eased that fear when he crawled to my side and pulled my body to his. I could feel his warm breath glide across my face while he held me in his arms. The longer we sat shivering in the snow, the harder it was to concentrate. I wondered how long this would last. Could our bodies shrug away the cold—or would we freeze to death in hell? I swallowed, trying to wash the taste of salt and fear from my mouth.

"W-W-Where do w-we go n-now?" I asked with a chattering voice.

Finn nodded to the red mountain in the distance while he helped me up from the snow.

"We must keep our bodies moving," Finn mumbled.

I nodded my head in consent. Finn released his grip from around my waist and faced me. My lips quivered while his gaze locked with mine. I tried to hide my fear and anxiety, but he saw right through the facade.

"We can do this." He gently brushed a strand of wet hair away from my face and continued. "We will find your aunt, and we will leave this place."

"H-How w-will we know what to do when we reach this place?"

"You know the book of poems and scripture by heart. All the answers are there," he said.

"But—" I tugged the book from my side and flipped it open. "I don't know what it means."

"You will."

I bit my lip to silence the chatter and then took a step forward into the unknown.

We trudged through the knee-high mounds of snow for seemingly hours, but in reality only minutes passed. This was true hell. A shrill howl came from the wind while we plunged through the never-ending white mounds. The wind and snow were numbing. I could no longer feel my feet, and the numbing sensation was moving into my calves.

A deep silence fell over the snow, and the ground began to shake under our feet. Finn looked at me—surprised. We stood like figurines and watched as the snow began to shrink around us.

"What's happening, Finn?" I glanced at the melting snow all around our feet.

"I don't know—hold on to me." His grip on my hand tightened. "This doesn't look good."

We stood frozen, watching the thick snow that surrounded us turn to pools of slush. In only seconds, every inch of snow had evaporated into the new, rocky ground. The ground shook again. The rock began to shift and crack underneath us. Steamy water began to bubble up and separated the ground into floating, shifting plates of rock.

"We've got to get to that mountain—come on." Finn tugged at my hand as he jumped over a large, bubbling crack to the next plate of rock. I followed.

The rocks knocked against each other with every step. Soon we found ourselves skipping from one rock to the next, bobbling up and down over the warm water. My feet and legs tingled as the steam and heat from the water began to thaw my limbs. The ground rumbled again. This time the cracks split wider between the plates.

My eye caught a glimpse of something darting in thc water. I paused and jerked at Finn's arm abruptly.

"There's something down there," I said. I bent down to take a closer look. I could feel the steam sticking to my face.

"We don't have time—come on, Clara!"

As he pulled me away from the steam, a triangular head the size of a beach ball shot out of the water like a missile. We both toppled backward, falling over each other on the rock. The black head bobbed back and forth on the surface of the water, hissing and staring straight at us. Its oval eyes glared with a scarlet hue, while a long v-shaped tongue slid between its two fangs. Finn slowly stood up and positioned his body in front of mine. The snake began to rise out of the water. *I hate snakes.*

The tip of his sword sliced straight through the middle of the creature's eyes. Blood gushed from the damaged head, while the split corpse fell to the plate of rock, like a limp rope. Just as Finn shoved his bloody sword back into its sheath, the body of the snake began to hiss again. Finn pushed me further back from the body and placed his hand back on the hilt of his sword. We watched in horror while hundreds of angry snakes spewed from the body of the dead snake. There were too many to kill.

"Go—go!" Finn shouted.

We leapt from plate to floating plate—we ran until there were no more snakes or cracks in the ground. And then we stopped to breathe.

"That…was…disgusting," I said as I tried to catch my breath.

"I agree. Are you all right?"

"I will be…I just hate *snakes.*" My skin crawled as I said the very word.

"It will be okay…They are below—we just have to stay above water and away from the cracks," he said.

"Good idea."

I saw a half grin when he chuckled. "Great idea."

We marched on until we reached the mountain.

We stood staring straight up at the height of the stone peak. The massive obstacle stretched hundreds of feet high, reaching up to the angry red sky above us. The rock was the blackest of black, but gave off a red appearance. I glanced over to examine Finn's expression—and from what I saw, I could tell that he didn't know where to go from here. I honestly didn't know myself—all I knew was that we needed to be on the other side.

He looked at me. "So, we climb?"

I didn't answer. A memory had popped into my mind. There was a story Fergus had told me long ago in the library…something about a mountain. I couldn't remember exactly. I finally closed my eyes and then let my mind wander.

In my mind I could hear Fergus telling his stories. *"There is a place—a most dreadful place. It tears at your beliefs and all understandings. Nothing is as it appears in this place. It is here that your fear can become reality and reality can become your fear. You must know what you believe—hold strongly to your faith. Then you can move mountains."*

"Clara—" Finn said.

I opened my eyes and glared straight into the mountains. The story was about this place. It was about these mountains.

"We're going through," I said confidently.

I squinted, and focused as hard as I could, until the mass of rock became a blurry sea of red. In the past few weeks, I had witnessed all kinds of impossible things become possible. If fallen angels could roam the earth and caves could transport you to a different world—well, then this must be possible. *This is possible.* I imagined the blurry rock splitting, like the raging Red Sea in the bible. My vision was so clear—I could see the violent waters part. I could smell the salt in the air. I could hear the roar of the sea.

I could hear a whisper of Finn's voice coming from behind—I fought the urge to open my eyes. Instead, I walked forward toward the sound of the water's hiss. I put all of my energy into staying focused on the wall of sea and walking through it. I could feel humidity sticking against my skin as I walked to the opening in the water. I took one deep breath and then stepped inside the sea. Two hands quickly took hold of my shoulders and spun me around. I opened my eyes. We were in.

"How did you do that?" His face was full of questions.

"Well, I…I don't know how to explain."

"It was amazing—the mountain just cracked. It…it…parted…It just opened right up for you." I watched the expression of his face jump around as he looked to me for answers.

"I imagined it to be true, that's all." As I spoke, I looked around and was a little surprised myself. To my left and right were cold black walls of stone. We were standing in an opening that was wide enough to be a two-lane highway.

A small fear popped into my mind before I had time to stop it. *What if we get lost inside this mountain?* Immediately, the opening we had entered turned into another stone wall. We were sealed in.

We both looked forward simultaneously. The one path that had been here earlier had turned into a multitude of paths. The mountain had become a labyrinth.

"Oh, Finn—" I moaned. With one quick glance from him, I could tell that he knew what I had done.

"We can't forget what Fergus told us," Finn said.

"I know," I continued. "Don't let your fears take control, and don't trust what you see." I could tell that Finn was pleased that I had paid attention.

"The idea of getting lost just popped into my head," I confessed. "I couldn't stop it."

"I understand—but it is important that we prevent fear from entering our thoughts."

"That's easier said than done," I said as I stared up into the red of the sky.

Finn started to take off down one of the main paths. I followed while curiously scoping out the walls of the maze. We walked several miles in silence before coming to the first split in the path. We decided to go right.

This course took us deeper into the labyrinth, twisting and turning, dividing into more paths the further we walked. The more I worried we wouldn't make it out, the more the path divided. But then something happened. As I looked up at the walls around us, I saw faces in the stone. There were hundreds—no, thousands—of faces staring back at me from the black stone. I quickly picked up my pace so that I was walking side by side with Finn. I tried my best to forget about the images. *None of it is real,* I told myself. I knew I needed to control my fear, but I could feel it taking control. I dropped my gaze to the ground, hoping to clear my mind, but now the stones on the ground were beginning to form shapes. I was losing it.

"Finn—we've got to get out of here, fast."

But it was too late.

The ground rumbled below us, showering us with loose rocks. More faces formed, gnarling at our feet. High-pitched screams filled the pathway.

"Clara—what's happening? What are you thinking?" Finn asked.

"I'm sorry, I'm trying to stop!"

The walls appeared to move around us. Paths were closing off, one by one—it looked like the mountain was going to close around us. Finn shot one of his questioning looks at me—as if I was the guilty party or something. But it wasn't me. Not this time, I was sure of it.

"It's not me! I'm not doing this—what's going on in your head?"

The ground was still shaking. The rocks were jumping from the ground like Mexican jumping beans. The walls were moving. Howling screams were in the air.

"Clara—listen to me. Whatever happens, you remember the stories. Remember the scripture and the poems, and if things don't go as planned, you leave and get out of here." His eyes were piercing as he spoke. "You understand?"

I knew I would never leave him, but I nodded anyway.

All of a sudden, a hot blast of wind blew at our backs—the red sky slowly faded away, while the mountain turned into a dark hallway. I couldn't see anything. I reached out with my hands and whispered Finn's name. An eerie feeling came over me as my voice broke the silence. I stood still with my arms still reaching to my front and sides—I could hear only a faint sound of someone breathing in the darkness. Why was he not answering me? I called again—just breathing. I started backing up slowly and reaching again for him, until I bumped into the wall. Finally, I felt the comfort of fingers sliding around my hand. I sighed in relief.

"Finn—this is not the place to be playing games." There was no response. "Finn?"

I remembered the pendant and quickly slipped my free hand to my neck, then under the chain. When I pulled the pendant over my head and into my hands, the pine needles instantly began to glow. The bright blue shade of light instantly pierced through the darkness. I looked to my other hand and screamed. The fingers that held my hand so tightly were not Finn's—they were from the wall. I tugged as hard as I could to free myself from the hand, but the grip only tightened. I screamed again.

The wall and the ceilings displayed thousands of gnashing faces and outstretched arms—all clawing at me. I frantically tried to peel the long black fingers away from my skin using the pendant. The light appeared to irritate the skin on the hand, but the grip did not loosen. My efforts seemed useless. Another hand darted out from the wall and grabbed my free wrist. I squeezed the pendant, while both of my hands were yanked toward the wall.

"Finnnnnnn!" I shouted—my plea was loud and piercing.

More hands began to extend from the black wall, grabbing at my clothes and my legs. The dark, twisted faces in the stone growled as I was pulled closer to the wall. My heart was beating faster by the second; my mind was racing different directions. *Where is Finn?*

In a swift breeze, a sword flew through the air and sliced the arms that were clenching my hand and wrist. My hands were free from the wall, but the disconnected hands were still holding on. I quickly yanked them off and hurled them to the ground. The long, bony arms evaporated into the black of the floor. In another swing, the metal slashed off the fingers that clinched my clothes. One by one the fingers plopped to the ground and disappeared like the arms before them. In the final stroke, the sword plunged downward—the blade drove into the ground, taking the hand that seized my leg. I looked back to the floor—all the limbs were gone.

"I thought you were gone..." I looked at him with scared eyes and muttered, "I thought I was gone."

"I was just a little preoccupied with some hands down the hall; sorry it took me so long," he said as he flashed one of his gleaming smiles.

I grabbed his hand as quickly as possible, with no intention of letting go.

"What is this place?" I asked, confused.

"We are in the hallway of the castle," Finn whispered.

"How do you know?"

"This was my fear." He let out a strong sigh.

-25-

MIRROR, MIRROR

THERE WERE TALL STANDS WITH BURNING CANDLES PLACED at the end of the dark hallway. Once we passed the candles, we entered a room filled with the strong feeling of death. The floor, ceiling, and walls were a polished black stone. Everywhere we turned, we could see our blurry reflection looking back us. A square chandelier dropped from the black ceiling. Two women dressed in black shawls stood next to a throne; they all seemed to be a part of the stone wall. Victor sat proudly on his throne with his long fingers intertwined, resting loosely in his lap.

"Well, well…it is nice of you to join us. I've been waiting for this day."

In a blink of an eye, he was standing right in front of me. Finn drew his sword and hurled it forward at Victor, but the blade stopped inches away from his throat.

"That's no way to treat your host." Victor smiled, and then nodded his head.

With a blank stare, we watched as Finn's sword went spiraling upward in the air. The sword spun until the point of the blade balanced on the ceiling, next to the chandelier. Suddenly, I heard Finn gasp and looked just in time to see a rope thrown around his neck, pulling him into the shadows of the room.

"I told you it would be easier if we were friends." The voice was haunting coming from the dark. *Erik.*

Finn wrestled, throwing one elbow back after another, but as the rope tightened, his efforts were useless.

"Finn," I cried.

Before I could run to him, Victor's eyes locked with mine. It was the same mesmerizing stare Edmund had used to leave me intoxicated. His aura grabbed me like a black panther going in for the kill. I could hear Finn struggle from behind, but I couldn't move. I was paralyzed in Victor's trance.

"I have the answers you seek," he said.

I unintentionally followed him like a lost puppy to the corner of the hall where a scarlet cloak was draped over the surface of a tall, wide object, resting on a stand. The cloak was the same as the one I had followed into the cave. For a moment, that thought broke his trance.

"Where did you get this?"

"From you, my dear." He grabbed the red fabric and flung it high in the air. I watched as the scarlet material rained down through the air, elegantly collecting on the floor in a red puddle. He motioned to the newly exposed surface of a black mirror. Through the deep black of the surface, I could see my own reflection, staring in confusion.

"Look—look deep into yourself," his voice commanded.

"Don't listen to him. Look away," Finn said with a pleading tone.

It was already too late. I watched as my own reflection turned against me. I could hear no sound from the hall, only a faint whisper in my head. A blurry image of a child appeared—the same girl I had chased once before. The girl from my dreams, the girl from the cave—we were one and the same.

I slowly stepped toward the mirror. The golden decorated edges were completely out of focus now. I couldn't take my eyes off the girl. As I neared the mirror, I reached out to touch the surface, just like I had once before. It was smooth, cold, and very much real. Instead of the image disappearing, like it had when I touched the mirror at Maytide's, the girl started to appear more in focus. Blurry images swirled around her. Bright strands of green grass formed below the girl's feet, and then long-stemmed daisies popped from the ground. I watched, dazed, as the young girl skipped and twirled through the field of daisies—I suddenly could remember everything.

These were images from my life—through my own eyes. The memories I had searched for were finally right before me, playing like a perfectly directed movie.

I placed my other hand to the black glass. A tall, handsome man, with bright eyes and dark hair, appeared holding the hand of a beautiful woman. I knew their faces right away—my parents. I felt my face tighten while I tried to hold back tears of undeniable joy. I watched as the small wrinkles around my dad's eyes smiled at my mother. My mom's blonde hair was flying in the wind—her wheat-colored curls danced and shimmered in the light, like branches of pine needles from the enchanted forest. Her skin was bright and flawless in the sun.

The images jumped to another moment from my life.

I was a little older, running around a castle playing hide-and-seek with a boy. He always found me, no matter where I was hiding, and he would grab my hand every time. I could remember it all. Finn. This image quickly faded, while another one appeared.

I was a teenager, and my father was teaching me how to use a sword. His eyes were so kind, and he smiled a proud smile as I learned the forms. He called me his little angel. I watched an image of him holding me tightly in a fatherly embrace, and I could smell the rich scent of pine on his skin—it felt like he was right there with me.

My mother came into focus. She sat by a fire, rocking back and forth in a wooden chair. She looked so happy, so beautiful. I remembered her smile, her tender hands, how every night she would kiss me on the cheek and whisper, *"Dream of daisies, my sweet child."*

Another memory emerged. A teenage boy walked along the water's edge skipping stones and yelling my name. I ran to him, giggling and twirling a white nightgown around my waist. I was wearing a scarlet cape.

He pulled me near. "Promise you'll never grow tired of me, Clara."

"That would be impossible. Things will never change between us," I promised.

The dashing young Finn placed a hand in my hair, then leaned in to press his cheek to mine. A simple embrace, but I could feel the love in my soul as I watched him pull away.

"Clara, I love—"

A loud explosion broke free in the night, sending us into an unexpected panic. The happy moment was lost.

We were running from the water of the ocean—running to the castle. Everyone was screaming—the castle was being invaded.

I watched helplessly from the mirror, feeling the fear I had felt at that exact moment. My breathing quickened, and I pressed my palm to the glass—wishing I could break through to help. Hundreds of men, all with swords drawn tall, paraded through the castle entrance. There were not enough men to stop them—my father and the crusade had been off fighting a war in the north. There was no one left to fight, the intruders had known. It was an ambush.

Finn grabbed my hand and led me to the side of the castle. Together we slid a stone out of place on the outermost wall and snuck into the castle through a secret tunnel. We quickly made our way to his brother's room. No one was there. We crawled through another tunnel that led to where my mother was staying—she was gone. I remembered praying that she had gotten away in time. We continued down the tunnel and jumped into a small opening that led to a vent in the king and queen's room. Through the holes of the vent, we watched as dozens of men surrounded his mother and brother. The queen held his young brother tightly as the men tore the room apart. Finn tried to call out to her, but I quickly placed my hand over his mouth. While the men grabbed items from the room, the queen's eyes looked to the vent. She knew we were there, watching. Sadness like no other had filled her eyes; she subtly motioned with her hand for us to stay in place and mouthed three little words, *I love you.*

A man dressed all in black entered the room with a crown in his hand. Victor. "Don't make the same mistake as your husband. Kneel and give your souls freely to me. In return, you will live a life like you've never known."

The queen slid Finn's brother behind her. Through her tears she found the strength to face him. "Our souls belong to the one true God. We will never bow to you."

Victor stepped up to her and slid his glove down her neck to her chest. She pushed his hands away.

"Such a pity, you would have been a beautiful addition," he said.

In one swift movement, the end of his sword went through the queen's delicate gown and out into her son's chest. They both fell limp to the floor.

"Say hello to your God for me." He grinned a devilish grin and walked away with blood dripping from his sword. Like puppets, the men followed their master.

Finn kicked down the wooden screen, and we ran to them. But they were already gone.

I could feel the sadness and the hate burning inside of me as I watched through the mirror—helpless once more.

The vision faded to another.

"Take this," Finn said, closing my fingers around his cross pendant. "I love you, Clara."

I was suddenly being pulled away from him. Blood ran down his side, soaking his clothes. His hand was pressed to his chest as he stumbled back on a balcony.

"No! No!" I screamed.

Finn struggled, but managed to stay upright to face his dark enemy. Victor paced in front of him with his bloody sword by his side, speaking words that I couldn't quite hear over a ringing in my ears. He forced Finn's body against the rail of the balcony, so hard I could barely watch, and then, with one fluid motion, Finn was cast from the edge.

Victor dragged me, kicking and screaming, to the grand hall of the castle. Edmund stood in the middle of the room with his hands reaching out to greet me. Victor handed Edmund a crown and shoved me into his arms.

"You did well. You have earned this crown—and here is your queen."

Victor smiled and then trotted off down a passage in the castle.

"What have you done?" I cried.

I beat at his chest over and over, yelling and screaming at the top of my lungs. His arms were tight around my waist, pulling me in so that I couldn't escape.

The image dissolved and another appeared.

There was fire everywhere. I ran down the hall of the castle, spreading flames while I screamed for all that I'd lost. I only had minutes before I would start to lose my memory. I had to act fast. Edmund caught me before I could finish the deed, before I could completely destroy everything. He knocked me to the wall as if I weighed nothing. My head was pounding, and my ears were ringing again. This time the pain was so intense that I couldn't fight back.

Then I was flying through a red door on to a bed. He left me there—he knew I would forget soon, that I would be his. But that was his mistake; I had other plans. I stood on the rail of the balcony now, looking down into crashing water. While my mind clung to the remaining memories of Finn, I stepped off the rail of the balcony and fell through the night air.

The images faded once more. My almost lifeless body was floating to shore. Fergus's face appeared, leaning down to pull me from the sand. He carried me. He saved me.

His face quickly dissolved in the mirror, until the mirror was back to its original state of blackness. All I could see was my own reflection, now crying.

My emotions soon turned angry—angry for the years I had lost, the love I had forgotten, the life that was stolen away from me. I snatched the candelabra that had been resting on a pillar to the right of the mirror and pounded the metal into the glass. I screamed through the tears as the glass shattered all around me. I did not notice or care about the small pieces that sliced into my skin.

Victor screamed, "Damn you!"

I threw the candelabra at his head, but with one quick motion of his hand, it dropped straight to the stone floor. He made another motion in the air with his hand, and my body lifted and then began to float in the air toward him. My lack of control over my emotions and fear made me his puppet.

Finn yelled again, "Leave her alone!"

"Isn't this precious? Young love."

"Take me! Take me instead—leave her!" he screamed.

I turned my head to catch Finn's adoring stare. My secret passion grew for him—stronger, and then deeper, as I floated helplessly in the air.

"I wanted to tell you, Clara. I wanted to tell you everything." His voice faded as Erik pulled at the rope around Finn's neck.

I could feel a cold air wrap around my chest, causing each breath to become a struggle.

"Let's get you dressed for the occasion, shall we?"

The cold air coursed the entire length of my body while I was suspended in air. The force of the air spun me around—my clothing and sword fell to the ground. I watched my blurry reflection from the shiny black stone above his throne as a black velvet corset appeared from nowhere. The V-neckline was edged in red velvet and rubies. My pendant lay hidden just under the lining. I gasped as the corset wrapped around my body and air weaved the lacing in the back and fastened the front. Black net and lace emerged over the corset and camouflaged my exposed abdomen. In seconds the netting was sprinkled with sparkling diamonds. As the cool air worked its way down, a bustling of red silk gathered at my hips and dropped just above my knees. The dress was beautiful, yet appalling.

"Stop!" Finn groaned.

"But she is not yet ready." Victor chuckled.

As Victor smiled, I felt the cold air wind through my short hair. The air tugged and twisted until my hair was away from my face. Then, out of thin air, sparkles dropped down—I glanced up to see the rain of sparkles shape into a diamond headpiece that formed a pair of wings. The wings were placed in my hair, and then a matching choker of diamonds wrapped around my neck. As soon as the jewelry was snapped into place, my skin became paler than I had ever seen, my lips turned blood red, and a shadow fell over my eyes.

"Your fear and your doubt pleases me," he continued. "Your soul is weakening. I think this calls for a little celebration."

He waved his hand, and the room instantly filled with hundreds of people dressed in fancy black clothes. There was another gesture of his hand. The curtains from around the room began to drop like flies, exposing dozens of mirrors.

"Look at your beauty—just like your mother." His eyes scanned my body from head to foot. "You belong here with me."

Air forced my floating body to the wall of mirrors; sadness filled my heart as I saw a reflection of myself dressed in the garments of his taste. He stood behind me looking pleased at what he had created—he smiled while he hooked diamond earrings into my ears. It was hard to recognize the pale face looking back at me in the mirror. I felt lost.

I looked to Finn. He was pulling at his throat, trying his best to keep his composure. Gorgeous women danced freely around him, smiling and laughing as if he were not there. There were men juggling knives—and a few exhaling flames high into the air. But then, I looked back to the mirror, and I could see their true reflection.

The room was filled with sad, soulless creatures. Their image of beauty had been erased long ago and was replaced with the reflection of disfigured humans. The men and women who were dancing had gray and withering skin and were twisting and turning about in burnt shrouds. Both of the men jugglers were missing their noses, and the men who breathed fire, well, they were missing their eyes. They were all his broken puppets.

I stared hard into the mirror at Victor and watched as his reflection of beauty began to fade. I watched his flawless skin turn gray and scaly, his pearly teeth turn dull and pointed, his eyes turn black and angry, and his long locks of hair turn white and wiry. I tried to pull away

His flaky lips smirked. "So it *is* true? Why...this is quite delightful. You can see what others cannot. I can see why Edmund wanted you for himself." He yanked me around so that we were face-to-face. Now

I was staring at a gorgeous face—the face of seduction.

"You will make a great dark angel." His hand grazed across my cheek.

"I will never turn!"

"Never say never, little nightingale."

He made a sweeping gesture through the air with his free hand, calling forth the two women from his throne. They immediately obeyed; throwing the shawls from their faces, they stepped forth to expose their true identities. Bleach-blonde hair tumbled from the first cloth, framing the slender face of a tall female. Her eyes were darker than usual, but her face still held the same proud smirk I had seen many times. *Lydia.* Behind the other dark shroud was the redhead who had chased me through the swamp.

"I should have known you were evil!" I shouted to Lydia.

"You should have known a lot of things," she replied smugly.

Victor snapped, and then both girls strutted past to one of the dark halls.

Soon, I heard the sound of rattling chains. Lydia and the redhead reentered the room dragging two reluctant caped figures into the light. The first chained prisoner struggled underneath the long black material and suddenly fell to the hard floor. Lydia forced the other prisoner to join.

Victor glided to the first broken human and lifted the heavy hood. I weakened when I saw her face.

"Mom?" I whispered. Her eyes moved from the floor to me.

She was beautiful—a blonde angel, exactly how I had imagined her. Wisps of delight were followed with spurts of fear. She was finally here, finally real. I could almost touch her. The remains of anger still lingered inside of me, but I could no longer act on it. I began to walk to her, but stopped in my tracks when Victor lurched over her with his silver blade.

"Where is your God now?" he questioned with the most sinister and evil look in his eyes.

"Clara." She was on the brink of tears when she spoke.

"A soul for two souls," he said. "You become mine, and I will let your mother and aunt go."

They say your whole life flashes before you just before you die. Now that I had everything back, now that I knew what I would see, I wasn't going to let him take it from me. Not again. Not without a fight. I looked back to his hard face and stared deep into the eyes of a monster.

"Be strong in the Lord and in his mighty power," I whispered.

He looked satisfied with my statement. He held his hand out to his side, and all of his puppets froze. I could tell from his reaction that he thought I was bowing to him, that I was giving in to his power.

"I'm ready," I said.

"Nooo, Cl—!" Finn tried to shout, but Erik would not allow for it.

Victor walked over to me, leaving my mother begging for me to stop.

"I have a gift for you," I said, trying my best to sound submissive.

The air that had rendered me helpless softly dropped me to my feet. He had released his grasp—I was finally free to move. I ripped the cross pendant from my neck and took a few steps closer to him. I knew that this might be my only chance. I could hear Fergus whispering in my head, *"The sword of the Spirit is the Word of God."*

I felt embraced in a strength that I had never known—a power that was far beyond this world and the next. It filled my soul. God was with me, even here in the darkest of places—my God gave me strength.

"The sword of the spirit is the word of God," I whispered. I understood now. My faith was all I needed; it was all that I ever needed. I shouted over the music and the laughter of his people. I shouted loud and strong. "My faith is strong—you will not reign over me!"

"We shall see about that."

He raised his hand and made the same motion that had lifted me into the air once before, but nothing happened. He waved his hand again in the air—nothing. I quickly tightened my grip around the metal cross, and the pine needles began to glow brighter than I had ever seen. The metal extended, wrapped in a vine of bright blue fire. A dagger. The answers had been with me all along.

I slashed at his chest, grazing the black vest that fit tightly around his shirt. He floated backward through the air to his throne, growling. He pulled a black sword from the stone wall and glared at me.

"You are no match for me, my dear. Grown men could not defeat me!" He laughed a dark laugh. "Your own father fell short."

I ran at him, attacking with an anger I had never felt. I lunged, aiming for his throat. The dagger hit his dark blade—sparks flew. I pressed all my weight into the dagger, but he was much stronger than me. I stumbled back to the floor under the pressure. I heard my name in the far background. I knew Finn was screaming, but all I could hear was a whisper through my thoughts.

I wanted Victor dead.

"Yes, yes. Strike with all your anger. I love it! You should be angry—your God has abandoned you, left you, just like your father. Oh, that is good, really good." He chuckled. "If you only knew how your father ran and hid like a coward. He would not fight me. He would not fight for your family! Doubt is an infection, sweet nightingale, and I feel you are infected."

I knew that he was trying to get into my mind, trying to plant that seed of doubt, but I wouldn't fall for it. I knew my truth.

"You are the coward! You are marked unwanted, cursed, damned! You are nowhere near as powerful as my God—not even close to a fraction of the power in his fingernail. You are merely a parasite roaming this world, infecting the weak. He created me strong so that you could not infect me! So that you could not deceive me! He created me strong so that when this day came, I would defeat you!"

Finn managed to knock Erik from his feet, freeing himself to run to my aid.

But I rose from the ground quickly, too quickly for anyone to see the power I had running through my veins. My head spun with adrenalin, but this did not affect my aim. No. I could see exactly what I needed to do and where my dagger needed to go. I knew Victor stood four steps in front of me. I knew I could reach him in one. I plunged forward and wrapped my arms around Victor's midsection, forcing my shoulder into his abdomen. Slowly we both fell into the hard, cold stone floor. I forced the dagger through his chest, piercing his black heart. I felt every inch of the blade cut into his tissue. I twisted the blade and then ripped it from his chest. He crawled backward from me to his throne—his body and mind still in shock. He grabbed at the wound while a black, tarlike blood pumped from the hole. The alluring beauty that had once hidden his true image contorted, and then disappeared.

He pulled his limp body up seven small steps to the seat of his throne, where his body slowly turned to stone.

One by one his puppets dropped to the floor—their twisted bodies becoming one with its dark surface. Lydia and the redhead took one look at Victor's frozen body before gathering Erik's body and disappearing down one of the dark halls.

The chains that were wrapped around my mother and Alice crumbled like dark sand. They came running to me with tears flowing down their faces. I couldn't seem to find the right words to say as we wrapped our arms around each other.

Our happiness was interrupted when a large boulder came crashing down from the wall. The boulders began to break, one after the other, like brittle sticks. A loud roar filled the space of the castle hall, and then water commenced to seep through the cracks of the unstable stone.

Finn stood behind my mother, looking down on us like a guardian angel, while the castle fell around us.

The water rolled over our feet with the purpose to push us out of the dark room. Candelabras extinguished from the water's mist—the hall was growing dark. This was all too familiar.

I noticed a sharp pain below my rib cage that burned when the water rolled over my body. I slid my fingers over my side, feeling a large gap in my skin. My fingers were covered in blood when I pulled them back. I felt more trickling down my stomach. With all the adrenaline that had been flowing through my veins, I hadn't noticed that Victor's blade had punctured my side. The pain was intense, now, pulsing through my whole body. I felt the color leaving my skin. I felt my energy draining from me.

"No, no, no." Finn's knees buckled, landing him right next to me in the water.

My mom and Alice followed his lead.

"How bad is it?" I heard my mother cry.

"We have to get her back. The wound is deep, and his blade was poisoned with the sap of the manchineel tree," Finn said. "It will take her soon if we don't treat it with arrowroot. The antidote grows in the jungle of the island. It can draw the poison out."

I felt his arms raising me from the floor. He cradled me in his arms as if I were as light as a rag doll and waded across the room to a hallway that was quickly filling with water.

"Come on!" he yelled over the sound of the rushing water. "We don't have much time!"

My head fell to his shoulder, resting in the nook of his warm neck. Water soon broke through the walls, destroying the castle with its immense power. And then we were swept away by it, pushed upward through a swirling hurricane, toward a bright blue sky.

The ocean carried all four of us safely out of Hades, to the white sandy beach of the island. My mom and Alice lay to my left, and Finn was to my right, hugging the warm sand the same way I did. The sun beat down on my skin, fighting the cold that inched its way through my veins. We were out of Hades.

The setting was even more beautiful this time around. The sky was brighter, the water bluer, the sand soft and white, but it all seemed to blur out of focus. My heartbeat echoed in my ear, beating loud and slow.

Finn leaned over me, shielding my face from the sun. "Clara," he said. His voice was like an angel. I felt his warmth as he pulled me closer to his chest. "Stay with me."

Even through the pain, I enjoyed hearing him call my name. I wanted to say so many things to him, but my lips would hardly move. He stroked my head softly with his warm hands, looking down into my gaze. I searched his mesmerizing eyes, finding paradise in their swirling sea of green. Slowly he lifted me away from the sand, until our foreheads gently pressed together. I could smell traces of cedar and the ocean on his skin now, a tantalizing fragrance I knew I would never forget. And then, while I still filled my lungs with every degree of his scent, he placed his lips on mine. Time stopped. It was as if a soft breeze swept away everything else in the world, leaving only the two of us on that beach. The surprise taste of cinnamon on his lips sent a warm surge through me that temporarily pushed away the aching cold. I melted in his arms as his soft lips pulled away. For it was in that kiss that I knew he loved me, and that I loved him; it had been him all along. He was the one who haunted my dreams with beauty; he was the one my soul desired. I stared at his glowing silhouette until my eyelids fluttered closed. I had lost him all over again.

-26-

LOVE LETTERS

I WAS SOARING THROUGH A TUNNEL. A PALE YELLOW LIGHT flickered in the distance. I was becoming alarmingly close to the light, but I didn't feel fear. I couldn't feel the weight of my body anymore. I couldn't feel the pain in my side anymore. I couldn't feel anything anymore. I was almost in the light. I was strangely at peace. Then there was nothing.

"Clara. Clara." A sweet voice echoed in my head. "Please wake up."

I felt something cool on my forehead. I smelled sweet honeysuckle. *Mom.* I felt something warm and rough cradling my arm. I smelled green earth and sweet-smelling aftershave. *Fergus.* I wanted to open my eyes to see them, but my lids still felt weighted. My brain told my body to wake—to move—but I couldn't shake off the undeniable tiredness.

When I finally came to, I was somewhere I hadn't expected. I was tucked comfortably in my frilly bed at Scarlet Heights.

"Sleeping Beauty finally wakes."

I looked over to see Fergus sitting next to the bed in a tall metal chair.

"How long have I been out?"

"About five days," he said.

I suddenly panicked, seeing images from my last moments in Hades flashing across my mind.

"Mom and Alice—are they all right?"

"They stayed by your bedside until sleep overwhelmed them. They are resting now as we speak. I'm afraid you are stuck with my company until they wake."

I felt the anxiety evaporate from my shoulders.

"And Finn? Where is he?"

His face took a more serious expression before he answered, "He stayed behind, dear."

I looked away at the red drapes blocking the window, stung by the truth, wondering if it had all been an illusion. Wondering why he would leave me after we had finally found our way back to each other. Fergus rose from his uncomfortable chair.

"He left this for you," he said, slipping a folded letter into my hand. He carefully stepped toward the door. "He loves you. That's why he let you go."

With a nod he closed the door behind him, leaving me with the letter and my own thoughts.

I unfolded the rough paper slowly, praying that it held an explanation—praying that it spoke of his love for me, but all it did was break my already fragile heart.

Please forgive me. I can only live knowing you are safe, far away from Edmund and the dangers of this place. Wherever you go, you will remain in my heart, filling the emptiness left behind.

Know that I will always love you.

It hurt. I wanted to cry for him, but only a single tear escaped. My body wouldn't allow me to cry; it wouldn't believe what I had just read. Finn wouldn't leave me. No, not like this. I threw the sheets from my legs and stumbled to the window, hoping that something would bring clarification. I pulled open the drapes, to find something else.

A scarlet material rippled in the wind—something sat tall, hidden underneath its flowing color at the edge of the cliff.

I stumbled down all thirty-five steps on the staircase. I hobbled through the hall and the room separating me from my truth.

I stepped into the chill of evening, feeling the weight of the wind on my shoulders. The cool, salty air stuck to my skin; the grass crunched under my feet. The setting sun peeked through a large gray cloud, shining down on the ocean waves, highlighting its swells and whitecaps. *Has he come for me?* My aching heart filled with hope. The pounding pain in my side momentarily subsided. Whoever it was sat very still under the cape. I tried to keep a calm composure, but the closer I stepped to the edge, the more my heart raced inside of me.

"Finn?" I whispered.

Nothing.

I reached out and placed a hand on the figure's back. Hard. Cold. Stiff. A gust of wind blew past my body, whipping the scarlet cape high into the air. A frozen owl sat somberly, staring out at the ever-changing sea. Attached was a torn piece of paper with two elegantly printed words—two words that brought fear with them. *Forever yours.*

"But I will never be yours," I whispered, dropping the note down into the deep blue sea.

ACKNOWLEDGEMENTS

A huge thank-you to my husband, Clint, who never stopped believing in this story or in me. Thank you for a fairy tale kind of love and thank you for marrying me.

Much, much, love and gratitude to my wonderful parents and brother. I can't thank you enough for all of the love and encouragement you have given me through my entire life. Thank you for always being there and for loving me the way you do.

I am deeply grateful for the support of my entire family and friends. Thank you for cheering me on through this exciting adventure.

A special thanks to Josh Longbrake at StudioBrainchild for creating the perfect website and book cover. Also, Mike Strout, for taking my awesome author photographs.

And, finally, thank you to my facebook friends, twitter peeps, and blog subscribers for your supportive comments, tweets, and messages. You guys rock!

JILLIAN PEERY is the author of the thrilling paranormal romance, *PineLight.* She currently lives in Texas with her husband, Clint, and mini-schnauzer, Zoe. To learn more about Jillian, visit her Web site at www.jillianpeery.com.

www.ingramcontent.com/pod-product-compliance
Lightning Source LLC
Chambersburg PA
CBHW050925120626
46552CB00001B/46
9780983750727